MW01092836

ARCANE SOULS
WORLD

SPELLS
AND
SLIP-UPS

THE WRONG WITCH
BOOK ONE

ANNIE ANDERSON

SPELLS & SLIP-UPS

Arcane Souls World

The Wrong Witch Book 1

International Bestselling Author

Annie Anderson

Edited by Angela Sanders

Cover Design by Trif Book Design

www.annieande.com

For my readers. Thanks for the wild ride.

Don't tell me the moon is shining; show me the glint of light on broken glass.

— ANTON CHEKHOV

CHAPTER 1
WREN

I f fucking up were a superpower, I'd be considered a god by now.

This fact was no truer than right that second as I picked my way over the cobblestones on Factor's Walk, nearly turning my ankle in the process. Trying to right myself, I stumbled, knocking my shoulder into the brick façade, and nearly falling ass over tea kettle on the uneven stone.

It was as if the universe itself was waving a huge flashing neon sign that said I should turn around and never come back. Considering *who* I was and *where* I was, the universe was probably right, but I couldn't listen to the wisdom then.

Not with a life on the line.

The arcane side of Savannah was not a good spot for

someone like me. As the designated degenerate fuckup of the Bannister witch line, me stepping one toe into the hidden magical world was like slapping a bull's-eye on my ass.

Rubbing the now-sore spot on my skin, I gave myself a little pep talk.

Get it together, Wren. Ellie needs you right now.

As far as pep talks went, it was lame, but there wasn't much to be done about it now. Staring at my feet, I minced down the crooked lane, desperately trying not to fall again. Every tourist and their brother took a stroll down Factor's Walk at least once, the signs reminding them to watch their step. But if you stared too long at the walls, at the rows of historic buildings, at The Walk itself, even human eyes would pick up on the oddities.

Those nearly three-hundred-year-old bricks that had historians creaming all over themselves? Yeah, well, they were made of arcaner bones from the vampire wars in 1723.

That lane that should be straight, but wasn't? It followed a ley line—the former bloody battleground where so many lost their lives before the witches and wolves beat the vamps back.

Those little pockets of green in the middle of asphalt-laden streets? Those were portals just waiting to be used—put there by Fae and witches alike as a way to circumvent the bloody attacks that left so many of our kind turned or dead or worse.

Every part of the city I'd grown up in was practically built for arcaners—leaving me mostly stuck on the outside. But this particular section of town? Well, it had been off-limits to me since I was about ten.

No pity parties, Wren. You have shit to do.

Yanking up my big girl panties, I headed for the one place that might help me. Considering I'd already lowered myself to asking my mother—only to have her deny me—this was my last resort. Granted, what I was asking for broke about four arcane laws that I knew of—and probably a few I didn't—but I was desperate.

Ellie Whitlock was my best friend in the whole world, and she needed me. I'd relied on Ellie my entire life. She'd been my only friend in school, my only lifeline to a stable upbringing, and my only confidant in twenty years. We'd been BFFs since Pre-K—my mother making me go to school on the human side of town after an unfortunate incident at an arcane school when I was three. My fucked-up magic—or lack thereof—didn't affect Ellie or her family.

Hell, there were times I'd wished her family would have adopted me.

And now her mom was in the hospital and might

not make it. The thought of losing Mrs. Whitlock made me want to scream. If Ellie had been my only friend, Alice had been my only mom. My parents hadn't ever been what one would call attentive. Hell, most of the time, I was pretty sure having me had been an accident —the pair of them too busy with their own love affair to actually parent their only child.

You'd think my mother would want to keep the woman who'd raised me alive, right? *Wrong.*

We can't interfere in human business, Wren. You know better than to ask me.

Rolling my eyes, I plodded ahead, my goal in sight. The Azalea Apothecary was the oldest witch shop in Savannah, but it was also the most rundown. The faded sign was a single storm away from falling off the building, the rusted bolts hanging on by a thread. But word on the street was that Carmichael Jones was who you went to if you needed something off the books.

From what I'd heard—which was limited since I didn't exactly run in witch circles—Mr. Jones wasn't exactly a crook, but he wasn't exactly an upstanding gentleman, either. What he was for sure was a top-notch warlock who specialized in healings.

Whether or not he'd help me heal a human, though, was a whole other matter.

A shiver of unease raced down my spine as I

clamped onto the rickety latch, and I had the strongest urge to not go in. Honestly, if I wasn't absolutely positive any spell I tried to do would backfire miserably, I would have turned tail and run. My gaze darted up and down Factor's Walk, the sensation of eyes on me nearly making me lose my nerve.

Ellie and Alice need you. Get it together.

Gritting my teeth, I snatched the door open and marched inside. Azalea Apothecary was no better on the inside than it was on the out. Dusty tables filled with odd trinkets and half-full jars gave way to bookcases stuffed with worn tomes and mounds of junk. Piles of random objects occupied the corners of the room hoarder-style, while bundles of dried herbs hung from every square inch of the ceiling. A grizzled gray man stood near the back of the crowded room near an ancient cash register, an unlit cigar hanging from the corner of his mouth.

"Get out," he barked, crossing his beefy arms over his substantial belly. "Ain't no way I'm gonna let a Bannister tromp all over my shop. Who knows what you'll break?"

Not that half the shit in this hovel wasn't broken already, but still, tears prickled at my eyes. Gritting my teeth against the sting, I managed to stand my ground. This wasn't the first time I'd been kicked out of a witch shop, and given my history, it wouldn't be the last.

"Please," I begged, reaching inside my bag for the wad of cash. Ellie and I had planned on moving in together after college, but here we were two years post-graduation, with no apartment in sight. Unearthing the fistful of bills, I held them in front of me to ward off my ousting. "I can pay."

His gaze snagged on the money in my hand, and he licked his chops. By the looks of this place, Mr. Jones hadn't seen a paying customer in longer than I'd been alive. "What? You stub your toe or somethin'? I ain't wasting my time on no silly girl with a hangnail."

Don't back talk the healer, Wren. Don't do it.

"It's not for me, you judgmental ass. It's for my best friend's mom. Do you really think I'd be tromping through here looking for you if it was something I could fix with a nail clipper and a manicurist? I'm liable to get tetanus in this heap." Gnashing my teeth, I took a deep breath, doing my damnedest to not start screaming. "It's systemic organ failure. Can you fix that?"

Carmichael narrowed his eyes. "Your *friend's* mom. Not *your* mom?" A slow smile pulled across his lips, exposing yellowed teeth and a fair amount of tooth decay. "You have my interest. What class is your friend's mother? She a witch like you or..."

This was the sticking point. If I couldn't get him to agree, Alice had no hope. It wasn't like I could bribe my way into my mother's good graces or beg my father.

"Human," I breathed, praying he wouldn't make a fuss.

He simply blinked at me for a solid thirty seconds. "I'm sorry—what was that?"

Stomping through the piles of junk, I slapped the money on the counter before reaching into my bag for the second roll of bills. It was my entire savings. Everything I'd squirreled away to set myself up. It wasn't just an apartment I was getting. It was a chance.

But it meant nothing if Alice wasn't breathing.

"She's human," I hissed. "Are you gonna help me or not?" The bank teller had audibly squawked when I'd pulled every dime from my account, her face purpling when I'd asked for it in cash.

Carmichael reached for the bills, but I slapped his hand before he could get within an inch. "Are you helping, or am I going to have to go down to the River Walk and deal with them?"

The "them" in question were the Fae, and I had no intention of dealing with that sort at all. Ever. Making deals with the Fae was tantamount to jumping off a cliff with piranhas, sharks, and razor-sharp rocks at the bottom. Anyone who had ever made a Fae deal regretted it, and I wouldn't be making the same mistake.

Luckily, my poker face was top-notch—otherwise Carmichael would have seen right through my bluff.

"What you're asking for is illegal, you know." He pretended to contemplate the legalities while pulling at his long, grizzled beard. "Healing humans ain't rightly my business, but I do love a challenge."

Raising a single eyebrow, I waited for him to continue. Hemming and hawing wasn't a promise he'd do the spell, and until I got that, I wasn't letting him anywhere near this money. I'd learned this the hard way at least twice—more if you counted how many times I'd begged my mom for things, only for her to tell me she hadn't agreed to anything.

"Fine," he barked, crossing his arms over his big belly. "At least your mama taught you that much, though, I'll be asking for my payment upfront before I get started."

"Shake on it," I insisted, one hand still on the money and the other outstretched. "In exchange for ten thousand dollars, you will perform one healing spell on Alice Marchand Whitlock. *Today*."

Carmichael coughed, sputtered, and nearly fell over. "*Ten* thousand dollars?" he croaked, turning a little red as he pinned his gaze on the pile of bills I was protecting. "Hell, girl, for that much I'll do it right now."

He stood straighter, hitching up his pants a little. Then he waved his hands in a complicated set of movements, which had me backing away from the counter, money be damned.

"No," I shouted, waving my own hands in the universal sign to "Stop." "You can't do it while I'm he—"

The ground pitched, sending the piles of junk toppling to the floor. I quickly followed, landing on my ass as a nearby cauldron sparked to life. The contents of said cauldron bubbled over, hissing like acid as it dripped onto the dirty floor.

"What the hell is goin' on? You did th—"

But Carmichael never got a chance to finish that damning sentence. All at once, the windows of his apothecary blew in as the caustic brew caught fire. Dodging glass and the heat of the flames, I scrambled to my feet, racing for the shop owner.

"You have to get out of here," I yelled over the now-roaring fire. "*Now.*" It didn't matter whose fault it was—and if anyone asked, I'd say it was *his*—this whole place was going up faster than a damned tinderbox.

Carmichael swiped his meaty arm across the counter, scooping up the money in one greasy, grizzled paw. Then the bastard took off, the heavy man moving far faster than I gave him credit for. He weaved around junk toward the back of the shop almost faster than I could track, leaving me behind. Almost as soon as he was out of sight, the path he'd taken was blocked by flames.

Maybe it was the smoke inhalation from the now-burning junk, herbs, and tinctures, but it took me a second to realize I should *also* be getting the hell out of there.

Coughing, I stumbled through the room, tripping over something or other. I fell, landing on my hands and knees, my palms cut to shit from the broken glass littering the floor. Then, I wasn't on the ground anymore, I was hanging upside down over a man's shoulder, the light of the early spring sunshine blinding me.

Unceremoniously, I was tossed off said shoulder, my ass taking the full brunt of the landing as I was dumped onto a patch of grass. Struggling for breath, I hacked and coughed up the caustic smoke, the fresh air slowly but surely filtering into my lungs.

Eyes tearing, nose running, I was so busy trying to breathe that I barely noticed the man who'd saved my life until he was already turning away. I wanted to say thank you to whomever kept me from frying like a red-haired shish kebab, but before I could get out a word, he was down The Walk, weaving through the stream of lookie-loos.

"There she is, Agent." Carmichael's booming Southern drawl echoed off the high brick walls.

Turning my head, I spied the beefy shop owner pulling a harried man through the gathering crowd. Where he'd fetched an Arcane Bureau of Investigation agent from, I hadn't a clue, but it didn't really matter.

Before now, I'd managed to stay off of the ABI's radar, but as the agent barreled toward me, I knew those days were over.

Once again, I'd fucked up.

Only this time?

I might just be in deep shit.

CHAPTER 2
NICO

"*Less do another shot.*"

It was official. I was in Hell.

Staring at the redhead slamming back another shot of tequila, I contemplated exactly what I'd done in my past lives to warrant this punishment. Being stuck watching this walking fantasy of a woman swallow down the amber liquid was the highest form of torture. She was stunning—with legs I could see wrapped around my body, hair designed to be twisted around my fist.

And those eyes?

It was harder *not* to stare at her than it would be to simply take her. Not that I knew what I'd do with her once I had her. She was trouble, with every single letter capitalized and underlined.

Wren Bannister was the definition of a hot mess, and I'd never even spoken to her. Everyone in the arcane world knew about the black sheep of the Bannister family. The one who'd been responsible for more than her fair share of catastrophes.

Fucking with *that* witch would only destroy me.

Yet, the second I pulled her from the flames of that damned apothecary, her wretched curse became mine. Her touch, her scent, they burned their way through my very being until there was nothing left but the ashes of where my soul used to be.

But she wasn't my mate. *No.*

When a wolf found their mate, it was a link between two souls—one that could never be broken. Not even by death.

What she did to me—what her *touch* did to me—was the darkest of magics. It was lust and obsession and desire and a near-mindless need to keep her safe. It was her jasmine and honey perfume in my nose, and imagining what her gasp sounded like, and... I shook my head, trying to clear it.

There had to be a way to break her spell—*had* to be.

How was I supposed to find my true mate with her scent in my nose? How was I supposed to come into my full power as an Acosta Alpha if I was stuck being a spelled lapdog to an absolute train wreck of a witch?

With only a week until my thirtieth birthday, I had to get her out of my head. If I didn't... I didn't even want to think about what would happen if I was still obsessed with her by then. She had to have spelled me.

Right?

That's why I hadn't stopped following her since the explosion—or at least that's the lie I would tell anyone who asked. Hell, that's the lie I was still trying to convince myself was true. The near-constant fantasies I'd been having would remain a secret, too. Just like everything else I'd learned about the obnoxiously drunken witch across the bar.

"Iss no' fair," Wren slurred, making my eye twitch. This was her third time loudly complaining about her fate to the human friend at her side—a sentence she was damn lucky to get in the first place. "They said jail or ABI, and I said jail. At least in jail I can't fuck up. Thisss is *sooooo* bad." She dramatically thumped her head onto her folded arms.

After what she'd done, most people would count themselves fortunate to end up with a prison sentence —especially since the alternative was death.

But not one of the "blessed" Bannisters.

Her family name bought Wren more than a few favors from the ABI. It sure as hell hadn't been her parents responsible for getting her out of the mess she'd made. They'd left that girl high and dry after her arrest, cutting off any and all ties to their daughter. Still, her choice had been prison or a ten-year service commitment to the ABI—*if* she survived the selection process.

Funnily enough, even though she'd chosen prison, the tribunal shoved her into selection school so fast it made her little red head spin.

Hooking a finger around the neck of my beer bottle, I shook my head. It was bad enough that she was sloppy as fuck in a bar at damn near midnight on a weekday. But being surrounded by humans—humans I couldn't snap at or maul to death or pluck the eyes from their skulls for staring at her rack?

Yep. I was officially in the deepest pits of Hell, with Satan himself roasting me over a spit. And it was one of my own making, since I was the idiot who'd followed her to this backwoods human bar in the first fucking place.

Though, considering the last time Wren had waltzed into the arcane side of town, she'd blown up an apothecary, I supposed it could be worse. The place could be on fire. Maybe tequila shots weren't so bad— even if the bartender's eyes *were* glued to her tits.

My wolf paced at the back of my mind, aching for me to yank her off that stool and toss her over my shoulder. Jaw twitching, I took a gulp of my beer. It was either that or give into my animal. My wolf wanted to do far more than just toss her over my shoulder. He wanted his mark on her and...

Sitting back in the booth, I ripped my attention off Wren and focused on her human friend. While my obsession was downing tequila like someone was going to stop making it soon, her friend was smartly imbibing water. A frown puckered the human's brow as the scent of guilt wafted toward me.

It was rare that a human felt that much guilt unless they had something to feel guilty about.

"Iss fine," Wren slurred, propping her chin sloppily on her fist. "As long as it worked and she's fine, I don' care. I'd do it again if I had to. It coul' be worse, yanno." The redhead shrugged so hard she almost fell off her stool. My ass left my seat, and I nearly raced to save her, when she managed to catch herself at the last second.

Jesus Christ, she's going to give me an ulcer.

Reeling the upper half of her body to rights, Wren smartly took the large glass of water her friend offered.

She didn't actually drink it, though.

Instead, she waved the glass—half of the liquid sloshing over the rim. "To Alice," Wren shouted, startling most of the other bar patrons. "The bess bonus mom on the planet. May she live to a thousand."

Wren had been charged with setting the shop on fire

after she'd failed to procure a healing spell from Carmichael Jones. Something told me Jones had been lying through his yellowed teeth when he'd spewed his testimony to the tribunal.

"Thanks to you," her friend murmured, tears filling her dark eyes. "I can't believe you did it, Wren. I can't than—"

Wren waved off her friend's thanks—once again nearly flopping off her stool. "Iss no prolem. She'da don the same for me."

Gnashing my teeth, my wolf continued his pacing. Sure, Wren might have screwed up, but the reasons may have been justified. It was so much easier to think of her as a fuckup instead of an accident-prone do-gooder.

Not that I'd be telling my superiors at the ABI that.

No one—and I did mean *no one*—knew I'd been at the scene, or that I'd been the one to yank her sexy ass out of the burning rattrap that was Azalea Apothecary. Hell, if I hadn't been tracking a spike in dark magic, I wouldn't have even been there.

It had been the same dark magic that trailed her delectable ass like a puppy all the way through Factor's Walk, though I hadn't scented it around her since. And just the thought of me not being there that day made my stomach pitch.

Yep. Definitely getting that ulcer.

A pair of boots clomped to a stop at the edge of my table. "Well, if it isn't my old pal Nico."

Shifting my gaze from the sloppy witch, I shot a glare up at the asshole who was dumb enough to follow me. "What do you want, Wyatt?"

Sure, I'd known him since we were pups, but right then, his presence was not welcome. Snickering, Wyatt slid into the booth across from me, his massive head nearly blocking my view.

"I needed a favor. You weren't at your usual haunts, so I followed your scent here. Considering I saved your ass in Canada—*twice*—I figure this is less a favor, and more me calling in one."

Of course Wyatt needed a favor, and of course he'd track me down to call one in. Though, it hadn't been him saving me in Canada from a den full of angry bears, rather it was me saving him, but whatever. He'd tell me whatever it was soon enough.

"What I wanna know is—why you're out here in the middle of bum-fuck nowhere in a human bar? Sure, beer is beer, but..." He sucked in a breath through his teeth, surveying the place, "this ain't your usual spot."

My eyes scanned the room before landing back on Wren. It was as if her ass was a magnet or something.

"Well"—He chuckled, taking a swig of his beer—"I take that back. *I* know why you're here. The real question is—if *you* know why you're here. Well, that, and if you've figured out why you're watching that woman like she's a nice, juicy steak?"

Scowling, I peeled my eyes off Wren's ass. "What's that supposed to mean?"

Wyatt snorted, scratching at his three-day scruff. "If you haven't figured it out yet, don't worry. You will."

Shaking my head, my eyes landed on Wren once more. Wyatt talked out of his ass more than his mouth most days. I wasn't going to be dragged into whatever bullshit he was spewing.

Wren lifted her heavy fall of hair off her neck, piling it on top of her head as she fanned her skin—the smooth pale column leading down to her shoulders, the curve of her waist. In my almost thirty years, I'd never wanted to sink my teeth into someone so bad.

That thought had me wanting to slap the shit out of myself to try and snap out of it. Again.

She had to have done something to me...

Wyatt whistled long and low, yanking my gaze back to him. "What?"

"Hoo-boy, you are in trouble. That's the Bannister witch, right? The one who blew up Carmichael's place?" He took a swig of his beer, seeming to hold in a snicker.

"Your point?" I demanded, raising an irritated eyebrow. "And didn't you want a favor?"

Wyatt's grin went wide. "No point, simply making an observation. Just like I observed every other man in this bar staring at those two."

Yeah, I'd clocked that about two seconds after sitting down. Wren and her little friend had garnered a lot of attention from the dick-swinging members of the population, and it was all I could do to not rip their throats out one by one.

And again, it made no damn sense.

She. Was not. My mate.

"I'm aware."

And by "aware," I meant that while I'd been watching Wren, I'd also spotted a pair of yokels circle the pool table like sharks, their eyes pinned on her. Out of every other group of men in this bar, they were the only ones who had the oily scent of menace to them. They smelled like predators.

My wolf scratched at the back of my brain, begging to be set free. He and I both knew what the score was with those two. If they didn't approach them here, they would elsewhere, and I doubted they'd be nice about it.

Wren slid off her stool as she slugged back the last bit of her water. I had to give her credit—at least it was water and not tequila.

"Time to go night-night," she slurred in a loud

whisper—one that didn't take preternatural senses to hear all the way across the bar.

The plan was to make sure she got home safely, and then put my head in a bucket of ice or something to try and get her out of my mind. A plan that was quickly going off the rails as I watched the two men toss their pool cues on the table and chug the last of their beers.

Wren's human friend quickly settled the tab before slinging the drunk witch's arm over her shoulder and marching toward the exit. And just like I'd predicted, the two men hung back for less than thirty seconds before they followed the women right out the door.

Fuck.

I was up and out of the booth before the door closed, ready and willing to commit murder until an iron grip stopped me. The growl that slipped past my lips had my best friend snatching his hand off my arm.

"You aren't planning on doing anything stupid, are you?"

Gritting my teeth, I fought off the urge to smash my bottle over Wyatt's skull and toss his ass out of my booth.

"You're the alpha's son, idiot. And we aren't exactly in the best place for whatever it is in that fool brain of yours."

Why did he have to go and bring that up? If we were on

the arcane side of town, it wouldn't be a question, but so close to humans? I really hated it when Wyatt was right.

"They won't know I'm even there," I growled, amending the plan in my mind. Granted, the first one involved me ripping out their throats and dumping them in the river, so maybe the change was necessary.

Instead of following them out the front door, I strode to the back exit, careful to keep my speed within human limits. Though, once I was outside in the shadows, I stopped holding myself back. Rounding the greasy dumpsters, I caught Wren's scent—that jasmine and honey perfume that made me want to shove my head through a wall. Only it was tempered by the stink of stale beer and male body odor. The two humans had split up, circling the women in an almost choreographed move that told me they'd done this before.

If they were wolves, I could kill them without even so much as a slap on the wrist—pack law superseding ABI law on this one point. We didn't abide sexual predators of any kind, and murder was always a viable option for taking care of that problem. As their scent got stronger, my previous plan started looking better and better.

The world needed less men in it who'd hurt women.

It needed them broken and bloody. They were fit for nothing more than worm food.

Mate or not, wolf or not, I wasn't about to just sit here and let Wren get attacked.

Once again, though, I was stopped by a hand on my arm.

"They cannot see you. None of them. Got it?" Wyatt hissed. "I swear you're going to get us both killed if you can't keep ahold of your wolf." At my confused frown, he pressed on. "Your eyes are glowing, stupid. Keep a lid on your shit."

But they were getting closer and closer to Wren, a spike in desire cloying through the air as it made my stomach turn. Shoving Wyatt off of me, I snaked through the parked cars, keeping my body low. While hiding was something I was good at, I didn't want to right then.

Every instinct I had told me to run and bite and rend. They said to protect. To save. To make sure that threats were gone for good. Those instincts didn't give a shit about the law I'd agreed to uphold or the potential fallout. They didn't give that first fuck that this could all go sideways.

With my back against the grill of an enormous truck, I peered around the side. A wiry man was loosening his belt as he watched Wren's human friend struggle to get her nearly passed-out cargo into the back seat.

The likelihood that I would commit murder rose into the stratosphere.

"Ah, *fuck* no," Wyatt growled, finally echoing my thoughts. "Fuck what I said before. I don't give a shit if they do see us."

About fucking time. "Stay with this asshole. I'll get the other one."

In less than a second, I located the predator, his hand nearly at the back door to the little car. Belt undone, fly down, he clamped his oily fingers on the door handle and tugged.

The growl that slipped from my throat had him freezing, his shoulders hunching as he slowly turned to look. But he never got a chance to see me before I shoved his head into the roof of the car, knocking him out.

I might have craved his blood on my hands and his flesh tearing under my claws, but I still needed to keep my ass out of the fire.

"What was that?" Wren mumbled sleepily from the back seat as I dragged the filthy human into the shadows, the pitiful parking lot lights giving far more hiding places than likely intended.

Instead of sticking around, I hauled the dead weight

over my shoulder and headed toward the water. Killing this asshole wasn't on the docket for me, but that didn't mean I couldn't let a gator do my dirty work.

A moment later, Wyatt was behind me with his own unconscious cargo.

"Swamp?" he asked, and I nodded.

"Swamp."

Ten minutes later, the pair of us were up to our asses in marshland, but our load was a lot lighter. And if those screams that echoed through the cypress trees were any indication, there would be nothing left of those boys by morning.

"So, about that favor," Wyatt said, flicking a hunk of mud off his hand. "I need you to cover my next class coming through the pipeline. I have shit to handle that can't wait."

My boots squelched to a stop in the silty water as I shot him a glare. "What?"

Wyatt's grin made me want to knock the shit out of him. "I sai—"

"I know what you fucking said. Please tell me it's not—"

"The selection class that starts tomorrow? The one your little redhead is going to?" he finished for me, his smile only getting wider. "Why, yes. Yes, it is."

Wren going where I couldn't follow was my one

chance to get her out of my head—my one chance to break whatever hold she had on me.

One of the screams abruptly cut off, a gator likely dragging a human under. Wyatt's eyebrows waggled as I realized there was only one answer I could give him.

Fuck.

Selection school here I come.

CHAPTER 3
WREN

I really shouldn't have taken that last shot.

Just the thought of all the tequila I'd drank last night made my gut do a flip-flop. Why did I think drinking away my troubles was actually going to help? It sure as shit wouldn't fix this bus ride, that was for sure.

The sun seared my eyeballs through my sunglasses as I rested my temple on the cool glass of the foggy window. The sway of the vehicle was doing a number on my stomach as the bitter churn of late-night tacos gurgled uneasily.

The bus was pointed north to Camp Blue Ridge, the ABI's selection school from Hell. I'd thought getting caught was the worst thing, but the sentence for my crime was far more dire than I'd originally thought.

Personally, I figured jail would have been an easier time.

Even though I'd heard horror stories of ABI prison, most of them centered around having one's powers stripped. Since I had no power to speak of—unless fucking up spells was one—jail would have been a cakewalk.

But *nooooo. Not a Bannister. Prison was beneath us.*

As soon as I uttered the word "jail," the portly man in the spiffy robes and giant staff turned purple, and two days later, I found myself on this godforsaken bus trying not to toss my cookies.

The only thing going for me nowadays was the fact that Carmichael had actually done the spell as promised. Alice's health turned around almost instantly, the doctors calling her recovery a "medical miracle."

As long as she lived, I didn't give a shit if I had to do ten years as an agent. But if I was being honest, the likelihood that I'd pass selection school was slim. What kind of agent would I be if no one could do magic around me?

I doubted I'd last a day.

Someone somewhere was going to do magic, and then there would be a fire or an earthquake or a fucking lightning strike, and then I'd get tossed out on my ass and thrown in jail.

The bus hit a pothole, launching my stomach into my throat.

Yeah, drinking last night was the dumbest shit I'd ever pulled, and going to that bar?

We were lucky we hadn't gotten eaten by an alligator or mauled by one of the patrons. But after receiving my bullshit sentence, I'd needed one last night of freedom. Paying for it now hadn't exactly been on my to-do list.

Two hours later, we started puttering up the mountain, the awful switchbacks having me wish puke bags were a thing on busses. By the time the monster vehicle rolled to a stop, I was sweating and ready to hurl my guts up.

"If you puke on my bus, cadet, I'll make you clean it up with a toothbrush," the sour driver barked, eyeing me from his seat. Nodding, I yanked my bag from the overhead bin and rushed down the aisle.

Soggy cedar-scented air slapped me in the face as I clambered down the steps, the humidity of the mountain a whole other animal than the warm caress of Savannah. A mosquito the size of a fucking barn owl buzzed in my ear, and I ducked, swatting at the thing, unsure if I actually wanted to make contact with a bug that big.

"Welcome to Camp Blue Ridge," a tall man called, and I straightened so fast, both my head *and* gut started swimming. His blond hair and light features blurred as I tried to get my shit together.

Alcohol. Bad. Tequila is the devil.

A small group of us loitered in front of the navy-blue bus as more people filed out. Another cadet bumped down the bus steps, her gait far more elegant than mine. Well, until she tripped over a rock I'd managed to miss in my flailing and nearly took a header. Me and another girl dove to help, and all three of us ended up knocking together and stumbling to the gravel drive. Sharp rocks dug into one of my palms, breaking the barely healed skin.

Perfect.

Me—totally used to biffing it—got up first, offering my lone non-bloody hand to the closest victim of my magical fuckery, my cheeks burning. The laughs I got—when people fell down, it was usually comical—but the bitter stare from the man at the front made me want to crawl under the bus and let it take me out.

"Jesus Christ," he muttered, shaking his head at the lot of us. "When you're finished..."

Wincing, I gave him my full attention. *Off to a fabulous start, Wren.*

"Selection starts tomorrow and will run for three weeks," he barked, his face made of stone. "The rigors of the Arcane Bureau of Investigation are arduous. We expect the best and will not take anything less than that. Not all of you will make it."

And if he just so happened to be staring right at me as he said this, well, then, so be it.

"Once you pass through these gates, all magic will be nulled. This is for your safety, as well as to teach you how to survive without magic. In the ABI, you cannot rely on your abilities alone. You need wits and gumption and your training to survive in the world out there."

No magic? None?

A glimmer of hope bloomed in my chest. If there wasn't any magic, then I could just be a normal person for maybe the first time in forever. No backfires, no explosions. Shit, this was like Christmas.

"You are to surrender all weapons, charms, potion bottles, and electronic devices in one of our Amnesty boxes," he continued, his stance wide as he held his arms behind his back. What was that position called? Parade rest or something like that? "Phones, tablets, and allowed magical items will be returned to you upon graduation. However, if you are caught with anything

I've listed, it is grounds for immediate expulsion from the program."

The woman beside me groaned as she unzipped her bag and unloaded a freaking mountain of magical shit. Necklaces with pretty baubles, bottles filled with glowing liquid, and a couple of athames were all dumped into a TSA-style bin with the name F. Jacobs on it. As someone who'd never worn a charm—let alone would try to test my shitty luck with a potion—the only thing I had to turn over was my cell phone.

The man—an instructor, maybe?—narrowed his eyes at me as he studied my nearly empty bin. "What else do you have on you? You won't get another chance to surrender your items without penalty."

Confused, I shook my head. I hadn't even brought my e-reader with me, since I knew all my shit would be rifled through. No one needed to know about my alien romance obsession. "That's it. You can go through my stuff if you want, but of the things you talked about, all I have is a phone."

I doubted tampons and toiletries were against the rules, but who knew in a place like this? I held out my duffle, the bright-purple canvas sticking out like a sore thumb. Yeah, it clashed with my copper hair, but the color was so pretty.

But the surly man didn't take it. Instead, he just

clenched his jaw and jerked his head to the side to get me to move along. Reluctantly, I shouldered the bag and followed the other cadets through the giant gate. The thing had to be about twenty feet high, the hinges creaking as it opened wide.

As soon as my foot crossed the threshold, it was like a weight had been yanked from my shoulders. Instantly, I felt lighter, freer, more in control.

Was this what no magic felt like? Was this what humans felt every day? Just breathing and living without a constant worry that they might explode something accidentally?

"Sweet mother of Christ on a saltine cracker," the blonde moaned, her knees practically buckling. "What the hell is that?"

"Whoa, there," I muttered, lunging to grab her before she fell, only this time I didn't trip us all. "You okay?"

She shook her head, her face pale and clammy. "I'll be fine. I thought... They told me it would be like this, but I figured they were exaggerating, you know?"

I actually didn't know, but I nodded, anyway.

Hooking an arm around hers, I kept her in line, marching toward what the angry instructor called our "barracks." In reality, they were four small cabins with pitched roofs and cute little gingerbread-style doors with numbers on them. Everything appeared clean and orderly—a task that would likely fall to us once we got settled.

"Males are in cabins one and four," the man yelled from behind us, making each of us turn to look at him. "Females in two and three. Pick a cabin and a bunk— that will be yours until you leave. Unpack your gear in your lockers. School starts tomorrow, so get some chow and rest. You're gonna need it." His tone was sinister enough—especially coupled with the dreaded up-down glare he gave me—that I figured he not only knew who I was, but he'd picked his punching bag for the duration of the course.

Lucky, lucky me.

After giving us a paper map of the grounds, which outlined the training areas, chow hall, latrines, and off-limits sections, he pivoted on a heel, making a hasty retreat. His instructions left a bit to be desired, but considering he was now gone, I supposed I shouldn't complain. I had a feeling he'd be in my shit far more than I wanted soon enough.

"Come on," I muttered to the girl I was still holding up. "Let's get settled. Maybe after some food you'll feel better?"

Shakily, she nodded, snagging the bag she'd dropped at her feet. "Pick a number."

Since the majority of the women had already chosen their cabin, I pointed us toward cabin three. Inside were four wrought-iron twin-sized beds, the linens stacked at the foot of each mattress. A pair of tall lockers separated the spaces, each one facing their respective bed, forming a giant metal wall for privacy.

I picked the bed farthest from the door, the dark corner of the cabin only boasting one small window. The walls were mostly wood planking with an open vaulted ceiling. Luckily there were ceiling fans situated over each bed since there didn't seem to be any air-conditioning to speak of. What was also missing was a shower—though the small bathroom did manage to have a single toilet and sink.

Unloading my duffle, I situated my clothes in the pristine wall locker, utilizing the hangers for my jeans and coat and folding the rest in the two large drawers at the bottom. I stacked my toiletries on the shelves at the side, stowed my shoes, and I was done.

My buddy, though, seemed confused at the lack of space. She sat on her naked bed, staring at the locker like it might jump up and bite her at any moment. I sort of figured she could still be feeling the effects of the no-magic wards.

"Hey, you okay?" I asked, startling her out of her horror-filled stupor.

Her smile was tremulous, but she seemed to rally. "Fine, fine," she said, waving away my concern. "Sorry. I just have never seen a wardrobe that small, and I was mentally trying to fit all my stuff in it." She held out a hand. "Fiona Ja—" She shook her head, cutting herself off as she took her hand back. "Never mind last names. Last thing we need is to get into a witch family pissing match. I'm Fiona. Just Fiona. What's your name?"

At this point I figured it was rude to tell her I'd already gleaned her last name from her bin. The Jacobs witch line was one of the oldest—save for the Bannister one, of course—their power and influence a force to be reckoned with—and not all of it good. Instead, I simply took her hand in mine and shook.

"Okay, Fiona, Just Fiona. My name is Wren." Honestly, it was better to not say my last name, anyway. When people found out, they either already knew about my degenerate status, or they wanted an "in" with my grams. Considering my grams didn't even like *me*, people usually got disappointed in a hurry.

The clomp of booted feet clambered into the cabin, accompanied by the screen door slapping against the outer wall. Fiona and I peeked around the wall locker to greet our cabinmates, the pair of them appearing tired and surly. One was green-haired and impossibly tall, ducking under the trim as she entered. I didn't know what class she was, but if I had to guess, I'd say ghoul.

Ghouls didn't typically join the ABI—or any other organization to speak of—mostly because their nest king or queen preferred keeping them in check. They were the tallest brand of arcaner—either born or made —and typically the crankiest, most destructive, and most whispered about, since they usually kept to themselves.

The woman following her was the ghoul's complete opposite. Her inky hair was pulled into a severe bun as she surveyed the cabin with disgust. Hell, if she'd have had a set of pearls at her neck, she would have been clutching them.

Fiona rounded the locker wall, approaching the two with a naivety that better suited a child. "Hi, I'm Fiona, and this is Wren. We chose beds already. Hope that's okay?"

The ghoul gently took Fiona's hand and slowly shook it. "Hannah. And that's cool. I like being by the door."

"Nice to meet you." Fiona's smile beamed as she moved to the uptight one, but she didn't take her hand.

"No offense," the uptight one said, her voice far kinder than I thought it would be, "but I don't shake hands."

Fiona's sunshine face fell. "Oh, well, that's okay. No worries. You got a name?"

The lady blinked at her for a second before shaking herself. "Malia. Sorry. I'm a..." Malia winced as she seemed to ponder the right word. "A psychic? Only I do psychometry. So, I try not to touch people or things with my hands if I can help it."

I couldn't hold in my wince. I'd read about psychometry oracles in one of my gram's books. Half the time they ended up batshit crazy or went to live in the woods alone, because they couldn't deal with learning every single thing about people from touching their stuff. I had a feeling those magic wards didn't help with a power like that.

Malia dumped her duffle onto her chosen bed, the sound of glass clinking making a damn racket. "Okay, unpack, food, and then we need to drink all the booze I brought before that chump decides that he meant to say we couldn't have alcohol, too."

Well, so much for first impressions, then. I'd sort of figured Malia would be an uptight goody-goody, and I'd never been so happy to be proven wrong.

An hour later, we were up the hill surrounding a decent-sized fire, a mix of arcaners on their semi-best behavior as they imbibed Malia's liquor. Her bag was filled to the brim with booze, but I was smartly drinking water, just happy to be invited. My red plastic cup rested on my knee as I listened to all the conversations.

People-watching was something of a hobby of mine. I liked trying to figure out what class everyone was and what powers they had. With no powers of my own, I loved learning about other people's magic.

To the right, a pair of mages lamented that they hadn't been able to produce so much as a spark from their fingers, resorting to starting the fire the old-fashioned way with a lighter someone had pilfered from the kitchens. A purple-haired guy was flirting hard with Hannah, even though he was clearly more than a foot shorter than her. Hannah didn't seem to care, though, so the flirting carried on, her cheeks as red as my damn hair.

Malia was talking animatedly with a pair of women that bunked in the other cabin, though she did it from a safe distance away to keep from touching anyone. She also didn't sit down, but she had donned a pair of elbow-length gloves. Fiona giggled with a few guys from cabin four, and I was sitting quietly on my log, trying not to smell the booze that permeated the air over the scent of burning wood.

Now that night had fallen, it was far cooler than I'd thought it would be, and I started rethinking my chosen outfit of short-shorts, an off-the-shoulder T-shirt, and combat boots. Okay, the combat boots were smart, but the shorts? Luckily, the mosquitos weren't so bad close to the fire.

Staring at the flickering flames, I let the conversations float over me. Well, until a man caught my eye through the fire. I probably should have noticed someone like him sooner, but with all the fuss and booze and buzzing banter, I had to have missed him.

Almost in the shadows, just outside the firelight, he stood with his feet planted in the leaves and his arms hanging loosely at his sides, his white T-shirt the only beacon, letting me know I wasn't dreaming. His hair was a dark tangle, sweeping back from his face like he'd ran his hands through it about a million times. But it was his jaw that really stole the show. Sharper than a blade and just as solid, even from here, I could tell he was in no mood.

Meeting his gaze across the flames, I nearly fell off my seat. It wasn't the fact that those eyes glowed in the firelight, either. No, it was the sheer heat in them that had me fiddling with my hair and adjusting my top. As dumb as it was—especially with a man seeming that pissed—I really, really wanted him to come over and talk to me. And if he happened to find me incredibly witty and blindingly attractive, well, then, all the better.

My breath hitched in my throat as my heart seemed

to want to thump its way on out of my chest. There was no way he was that pretty, right? No way he was actually as fucking beautiful as I thought he was.

Right?

The best I could do was toss my hair, but when I tried resting my weight on my hand—for added cleavage building purposes—I missed the log completely and slipped right off my makeshift seat.

With my legs in the air and my hair snarled in the leaves, I seriously considered crawling away and burying myself in the woods somewhere. Add in the fact that my cup of water was now all over my shirt, I figured dying was my only option. Surviving this embarrassment didn't seem like a good idea.

The hottest man I'd ever seen in. My. Life. Just saw me biff it. Now was the perfect time to just expire.

But no. Instead of dying right there on the spot, I heard a deep, silky voice ask the most damning of questions. "Are you drunk?"

Glaring, I met his amber gaze over the fallen log, my embarrassment tempered by his rude question. Though considering everyone else was drinking, maybe it wasn't so rude.

"No. My beverage—that I am now wearing—was water. I'm just clumsy, but thanks for the assist."

Awkwardly, I tried to disengage myself from the

brambles, but I wasn't having the best of luck. It was just my luck that I couldn't even die in peace.

"Here," he rumbled, kneeling next to me, "let me help."

His fingers made quick work of disentangling my hair from the bracken, offering me a hand up once I was free. I took it and he hauled me up with little effort. His hand was warm as it clasped over mine, his skin sending little jolts of adrenaline into my body. Up close, I noticed his five-day-old scruff of a beard that surrounded a pair of lips—

"You okay?" he asked, stepping closer, his voice doing very weird things to my middle as I stared at his mouth.

Stop staring at his mouth, Wren.

Shaking myself, I met his gaze and then lost my train of thought all over again when he gently pulled a leaf from my hair. Was I goo now? I had to be because there was no way I was acting like this. No, this was a dream—or a nightmare—and I would wake up anytime now.

But instead of extricating myself from the situation, I just. Kept. Staring at his fucking eyes. And those irises weren't only amber, either. No, they were the color of good whiskey, the firelight reflecting off them almost like a cat's.

Leave. Go. Dear sweet mother of all that is holy, get your shit together and walk. Away. Please.

"Fine," I croaked, my voice breaking like a teenage boy's. Cheeks burning, I cleared my throat. "Fine. Thanks for the help. I'm going to go back to my cabin and die now, if you don't mind." Reluctantly, I pulled my hand from his. "Tootles."

Tootles? Did I actually just say tootles? Someone kill me.

Nodding at the sheer embarrassment, I skirted around the hot man and marched double-time away from the fire. I heard my name being called, but I couldn't stop. Not even when I stumbled over a rock and nearly ate it. Again.

No, I practically ran, stumbling down the hill and praying no one followed me as I made my escape.

But escape was a stretch, wasn't it? Because I had three more weeks here, and I had a feeling I'd be seeing him again.

Whoever he was.

Touching Wren was a mistake.

But what else was I supposed to do? Just stand there while she tangled herself in the brambles? Be an asshole and watch her squirm?

Though, as soon as my skin made contact with hers, that pull that had been tugging on me since I'd yanked her from the flames, crashed over me like a tidal wave once again. I was supposed to be distancing myself from her, not getting closer, but I couldn't seem to stop myself from seeking her out.

I couldn't keep myself from getting closer to her, making myself known. I needed her to see me for some stupid reason—needed her to know I was there. And as soon as I locked eyes with her, I was lost.

Again.

How was I supposed to loathe the woman when she was that fucking beautiful? And the spark in those odd gold-and-green eyes—the way she blushed?

Gods, I was fucked.

The heat of her skin filtering into my palm was enough to make me want to sink my fangs into her neck and brand her with my mark.

She's not your mate, you idiot. This is just her spell—her power. Had to be... Right?

But when she practically ran from me with the scent of her desire on the air? Well, it had my wolf fighting against my hold, ready to race after her, even under these shitty null wards. It was bad enough I couldn't quite stop myself from following her through the forest toward her cabin. The lie I told myself this time was that I wanted to make sure she was safe.

There were predators in the woods, right? The magic and fences couldn't keep everything out.

And this was Wren, for fuck's sake. She needed a keeper.

But I'd been watching her all night, and it wasn't until I stepped into the firelight, did she start stumbling all over herself. Truth be told, that shit was fucking adorable. The flush to her cheeks, the way her heart fluttered like a hummingbird's, the way her pupils dilated.

And her scent nearly made me go out of my mind.

She slammed into her cabin, muttering to herself, not knowing I could hear every word. "How could you do that, Wren?" she grumbled, crashing against something metal. "The hottest man you've ever seen, and what do you do? Spill your stupid drink all over yourself. No wonder he thought you were drunk."

I pressed my lips together so I didn't laugh outright. It was tough to reconcile this version of Wren with the black magic witch who'd spelled me to obsession. And wouldn't a spell like that be dampened by the wards? Or was her magic like mine—unable to be controlled by nulling spells? Those spells didn't dull a single aspect of my wolf—my senses just as acute inside this facility as they were back home.

Which was why the shuffle of steps through the leaves had my eyes rolling. Sneaking up on a wolf was a ballsy move.

"So, you've picked your prey, then?" Ames taunted, likely trying to get under my skin. Chet Ames was an asshole of the highest order, and that assessment had been made before he'd ever even opened his mouth. His name was Chet for fuck's sake. It was as if his parents knew he was a blight on the arcane world before he ever left the womb.

As soon as I'd arrived, he'd taken it upon himself to

show me the "ropes," as he liked to call it. Even though my clearance was higher than his, as was my rank. Plus, this wasn't my first rodeo at selection school or covering for Wyatt. It figured that his inferior ass would follow me, though, why anyone in their right mind would try to sneak up on a wolf was a damn mystery.

Unlike him, I still had all my powers.

Ignoring Ames seemed like my best option. We did this with snapping pups all the time. And that's exactly what he was, nothing more than a yipping puppy with no damn sense.

"She is hot, right?" Chet said through a chuckle and my eye involuntarily twitched. "Though, I wouldn't touch that ass with a ten-foot pole if you ask me. Fucking Bannisters, tossing their power around at every turn. I still can't believe she got out of jailtime after what she did. I can't wait to toss her ass out of here." He rubbed his hands together like he couldn't wait to enact his plan. "After I make her suffer, though. She needs someone to teach her a lesson."

Gritting my teeth, I tried not to snap, keeping my eyes trained on cabin three's door. This idiot had no idea what he was talking about. He knew nothing about Wren or her family, and he sure as shit wasn't going to touch her—not on my watch.

But it also wasn't my job to defend Wren's reputation.

Not that my tongue got that memo.

"She chose jail, actually. And that family you hate so much? They cut her off. She probably hates them just as much as you do. Maybe having an agent in our ranks with the Bannister name might be the way to keep those assholes in check." I finally broke my gaze from Wren's cabin and loosened the leash on my wolf a bit. "But it won't be *you* tossing her out anywhere. Or making her suffer."

Especially since tossing her out would be a death sentence for her. I'd perused her intake paperwork and it was all there in black and white.

Jail wasn't an option for Wren.

It never had been.

Chet stumbled back a step. "Dude. How are you doing that? Even Cassidy can't shift here."

But I hadn't shifted at all. I'd simply let a sliver of my wolf shine out of my eyes. And the reason was simple. "I'm an alpha. Wyatt is not. Now run along and collect the others. The party should be dying down soon enough."

And as soon as the cadets were tucked safe in their beds, Hell Night would begin.

THERE WAS A BLISSFUL SIMPLICITY TO HELL NIGHT FROM AN instructor's point of view. It reminded me of stalking prey. All you had to do was wait until they felt safe and warm and relaxed, bide your time until they rested, and then rip it all out from underneath them.

The tough part was busting into a cabin in the middle of the night with a female ghoul right by the front door. It didn't matter what those null wards did, they didn't change the basic physical makeup of an arcaner. And a nearly seven-foot-tall ghoul was scary no matter whether she was hungry or not.

Naturally, I left that task to Chet, allowing his stupid ass to go in first and flip the mattress of Cadet Dumond. One of the last of her line, Dumond had likely fought plenty of arcaners just to stay alive. Chet was about to get his shit rocked.

Smartly, I stayed on the outside of the cabin, stepping to the side of the door once Dumond's growl rumbled from her chest. Two seconds later, Chet came flying out of that door, landing on the soft dirt in front of the cabin. He seemed dazed for a second before he peeled himself from the ground and marched right back into the line of fire.

"Everyone up," the idiot yelled, not realizing all four women were wide awake and already getting dressed. "Get your asses in formation. Let's *go*."

It took everything in me not to haul him from the women's cabin myself. There was no reason he should be in there in the first place. Regs dictated that only female instructors could enter their cabins after night-fall. But there weren't any female instructors here this iteration, so I had to go with it.

Squawks and distressed cries came from all four cabins, the clang of locker doors being opened, items being thrown to the ground, mattresses being flipped over.

Cadets spilled out of their cabins at the shouts of cadre, some scrambling barefoot to get in line, their ill-suited clothing choices likely about to bite them in the ass. The last cadet to leave was Wren, her red hair piled on top of her head as she hopped to finish tying her boot. She raced past me, trying to get into one of the two lines.

"It's marching time, ladies and gents," Girard announced, clapping his hands together. He was the oldest cadre member and likely the surliest. If I was stuck being the commandant of bootcamp from hell, I'd be pissed, too. But there wasn't much room in the ABI for agents that didn't follow orders—a fact I'd need to remember if I didn't rise to Alpha.

"Grab a ruck and a canteen and get back in line," Girard continued, his booming voice carrying through the trees. "Move."

The cadets raced for rucks, some testing the weight before attempting to choose lighter ones. Not Wren, though. She hoisted the first pack she grabbed onto her back before helping a smaller girl do the same, snatching up a canteen for her when the pack threatened to tip the poor girl over.

"No helping," Chet snarled, his gaze trained right on Wren. "Worry about yourself and your own pack and get your ass back in line."

Wren nodded and moved to obey him, stumbling around other cadets as she tried to return to the line.

"Get your ass in gear, cadet," Chet yelled, planting a hand in her rucksack, and shoved.

Wren stumbled, managing to catch herself before she fell, but her canteen went flying, landing with a *splat* in a puddle. She reached for it, but Chet was there again, shoving his soon-to-be dead hand against her bag. This time Wren did fall, landing on her hands and knees in the mud.

The growl that ripped up my throat was involuntary, the quiet snarl alerting every single arcaner with acute hearing of my displeasure. Wolves did not harm women—not *ever*. Warlocks, on the other hand, had a long history of doing unspeakable things, no matter the gender.

"I said move, cadet," Chet shouted, bending down so his wide-brimmed campaign hat was right in her face, *tap-tap-tapping* on her forehead as she struggled to get up with fifty pounds strapped to her back.

I figured it was high time for Ames to have a different job, or maybe it was about time for him to stop breathing altogether. My hand latched onto the back of his neck, hauling him to standing as I pulled him away from Wren. He was out of line, and it didn't matter who Wren was. Thick talons erupted from my fingers, pressing into the struggling man's flesh as I marched him over to Girard.

The death mage's eyes widened when he noticed us, but he kept his cool.

I... *did not.* "Either you teach him the right way to discipline cadets," I hissed under my breath, "or I will. You pick, but know this, he harms another student, and my lesson will be bloody."

No wonder Wyatt wanted me here. Covering for him had only been part one of his favor. Part two was sniffing out what the fuck was going on that had all the female instructors requesting transfers left, right, and center.

Girard had let this fuck get away with too much for too long.

"Noted." He tilted his head to the side. "You gonna let him go now, or am I going to have to bury him out in the woods somewhere?"

Opening my hand, Chet dropped like a rock. Good. Maybe he learned something from this experience. Though, he was so damn stupid, the likelihood was slight.

Turning to survey the cadets, I purposely kept my gaze from the far-left line, preferring to keep the brim of my black ball cap low. I didn't wear the traditional cadre garb, nor did I don that ridiculous campaign hat. But the siren call of her eyes on me was more than I could bear.

My chin tilted up, my gaze locking on those odd gold-green eyes. They widened, her luscious mouth forming into a pretty "O" of surprise.

Yep, definitely shouldn't have touched her. This was going to be a long three weeks.

CHAPTER 5

WREN

Pretty please with sugar on top, someone, somewhere please tell me I didn't embarrass the fuck out of myself last night in front of one of my instructors.

An instructor that I would like to maul with my mouth at the first given opportunity.

Of course I did. It was bad enough when I'd assumed he was a student. But an instructor?

I most definitely should have crawled into the woods and just perished.

Shaking myself, I snapped my mouth shut, pointing my eyes at my feet so I didn't get lost in his gorgeous gold ones. My mother frequently got onto me for "catching flies," but if she were in my shoes, she'd be doing it, too. Here I was muddy, wet, and already sweaty at the ass crack of dawn while the hottest, most unattainable man I had ever seen in my freaking life just stood there looking like *that*.

A black T-shirt stretched across his pecs with "Cadre" printed across them in gold. Tight on his biceps, the cotton strained against his muscles like it was in danger of ripping. The other instructors were in weird fatigues while he was in climbing pants, hiking boots, and a ball cap, his scruff working that jaw for all it was worth.

And he'd pulled that blond guy off of me—the same one who'd been so rude when we'd arrived. I'd sort of expected selection school to suck, but I hadn't quite wrapped my head around getting shoved to the dirt on the first day. I also hadn't expected to get some weirdo's hand in my face, poking my forehead like he was trying to pop a zit.

It was humiliating to say the least, but he'd simply strode over and picked that guy up like he was no heavier than a feather, frog marching him right on over to the angry lead instructor—who seemed all the way over it—holding up the asshole by his scruff like he was a naughty puppy or something.

Yes, my heart was going all pitter-pat, trying to pump its way out of my chest. I'd have rolled my eyes at myself, but I didn't want one of the instructors to think I was doing it at them. I was in enough shit already.

"Turn to your left," the older instructor boomed, making all of us jump.

I did as told, my pack bumping into Fiona's as she turned right by accident. Jesus, it was like a damn clown show. She nearly fell over, the pack's weight too much for her, and *I* nearly fell trying to keep her up. Without a word, I planted my hands on her shoulders and steered her in the right direction.

"March, ladies and gents," he called, and it was the start of a very, very long day.

IF I HEARD THE WORD "MARCH" ONE MORE TIME, I WAS GOING to smash my ruck into someone's face.

"Get your ass in gear, cadets. Let's move," the instructor, who'd finally introduced himself as Girard, called. And he'd done that announcement while we were all chin-deep in a trench, crawling under barbed wire with that godforsaken pack still on our backs.

The damn thing had to weigh at least fifty pounds, and the longer I wore it, the more I knew my back would never be the same after this. The blond instructor was Ames, and the hot guy with the impossibly gold eyes and the jaw from the angels? His name was Acosta.

It figured he'd have a cool last name to match his wide shoulders and fabulous ass.

That tight behind was the only thing keeping me going at this point. I focused on those rock-hard buns and marched my face off. I had blisters on my heels, enough bug bites to qualify for a malaria trial, and mud in some very unfortunate places, but I had a carrot marching in front of me and that was enough.

There were three other instructors: Haynes, October, and Pierce, but they mostly stayed on the periphery, herding us up this bullshit mountain.

Fun fact: the mountains in northern Georgia were a bitch. The biggest bitch known to mankind. They were awful and just mean. Filled with limestone and sedimentary rocks, I slipped more than I thought possible, the mud caked on my boots making them damn near pointless. Also? Push-ups were the bane of my existence. Struggling to heave my body off the ground while wearing a pack that heavy should be against the Geneva Convention or something.

My only saving grace was that I hadn't drank last night, because Fiona, Hannah, and Malia? Well, they were dehydrated, puking, and desperately trying not to pass out. Since I'd avoided imbibing, I was only ahead in the "not puking" department.

"Time for a water break," Girard shouted, and the

lot of us let out relieved groans. "Remove your packs, take a rest, and drink the water you have left."

The sun was high over our heads, the trees giving us plenty of cover but exciting the bugs something awful. There wasn't a salve in the world that would fix my itching skin, but weirdly enough, the mud had helped a bit.

Dumping my pack, I used it as a seat to keep my ass off the ground, and sipped my water. You couldn't pay me to chug anything right now, my stomach giving me fits. Everyone smelled like they'd rolled in manure—which we probably had—it was hot, and I was getting a headache.

Fiona and Hannah downed the last of their canteens, dropping their rucks as they wilted to the ground. Malia was still climbing up the hill, practically crawling the last few feet with a full pack on her back. She struggled out of it, rolling to her side as she caught her breath.

Out of curiosity, I opened the top flap of my ruck, finally able to inspect the contents after hours of carrying it. Inside were four two-liter bottles of water, a laminated map, a compass, and a plethora of dive weights. No wonder. I probably had bruises on my back from the ill-padded bag. I pulled a water bottle from the pack and filled my canteen, using a handful of it to wash the burning salt, dirt, and who knew what else off my face.

My eyes drooped once my face was clean, that small bit of comfort making me want to sleep for days. Every part of me ached—from my mud-caked scalp all the way down to my toes. I also had a sneaking suspicion my feet were bleeding, but I didn't want to take my boots off to check. We were up the mountain in the middle of nowhere, and I worried I wouldn't be able to put them back on again.

Several of the male cadets complained, their stomachs making them far more irritable than the rest of us. I wished there were some kind of rations in my bag, but I was too tired to get off of it to get a better look. Ignoring the complaints, I sipped my newly procured water and waited, trying to keep myself awake.

Trusting people had never really been my strong suit, but after the last day? I figured my wariness of the instructors was warranted. No one had touched me since Acosta pulled that dude off me, but I wasn't going to fall down at his feet in thanks.

Okay, so if he crooked his finger at me, I totally would, but that was beside the point.

By the time I looked up, it was damn near dark, and the instructors were nowhere to be seen. Alarm and a fair amount of adrenaline lit my limbs on fire, and I jumped to my feet, the ache in them tempered by fear. I hadn't exactly been paying attention to my surroundings while I was struggling to breathe, so I had no idea where we were.

The faint thrum of an engine drew my gaze up and to the right, the gentle glow of what had to be taillights peeking through the trees. Girard stood near the driver-side door of a giant pickup truck and cupped his hands around his mouth.

"The lot of you have until sunup to get back to camp. Any stragglers who don't make it back before the deadline will be cut from the program. Any do-gooders caught helping other cadets will be punished. The first ones back will get a reward. Good luck, people."

Then Girard hopped into the bed of the truck, his seat a suspicious-looking lump as the truck rolled away. A faint flash of army-green canvas caught my eye, and a pit of dread opened up beneath me. I knelt, snatching up my pack, the slight bit of reassurance needed to make it so I didn't start crying.

A few minutes ago, I'd hated the damn thing, but as my gaze flitted over the ground nearby, I realized just how lucky it was that I still had that damn lump of heavy canvas. Frightened squawks of protest rose from the other cadets, and my hand tightened on the strap. Girard had made it sound like helping others wasn't allowed. The last thing I needed was someone to steal it right off my back.

"Gods, what are they trying to do to us?" Fiona moaned, her hands empty and canteen hanging open at her side.

Those bastards had told us to drink all our water, stole all the extra, and then bounced out with no way home.

"Break us down," Hannah muttered, cracking her neck. "How are we supposed to be good little agents if we aren't obedient lapdogs first?"

Obedience had never really been my style, though. A few of the other cadets were already walking down the mountain, probably half-delirious from dehydration and would likely pass out after one rough stumble.

"Wait," I called to their backs, already regretting what was about to fall out of my mouth. "Does anyone else still have your ruck?"

Hitching the strap higher on my shoulder, I grimaced when most everyone shook their heads. Eight liters of water wasn't going to cut it for sixteen people. Plus, I couldn't remember the last time I'd eaten something. Or gone to the bathroom. Or slept.

"Thank the gods for that. At least they did us a solid and took them back with them," the purple-haired guy groused. "At least when I'm stumbling through the woods in the dark, I won't be carrying all that weight."

Jesus, Mary, and Joseph, they had no clue what was in those bags. "Those rucks had water in them. And a map, compass, and a bunch of other shit."

Those distressed sounds from before were nothing compared to the moaning I heard now. A few of the males' gazes laser-locked onto my ruck, a calculating gleam to their eyes as they stepped forward.

"Stop right there," Hannah growled, peeling herself from the ground to stand in front of me. "Take one more step and you'll regret it."

Peering around the ghoul, I met the purple-haired guy's eyes. "I plan on sharing so keep your panties on."

He frowned. "They told us not to help each oth—"

"No," I denied, cutting him off. "They said helping each other would get you punished. *You're* not helping anyone. I am. I'm the only one with a pack, map, or water. I say we get some light, some water, and figure out where the hell we're going."

Another guy stepped forward. "And what about the reward for getting there first?"

Rolling my eyes, I shook my head. I swear it was going to turn into *Lord of the Flies* soon if I didn't get these people some sleep and food. "I could have kept my mouth shut and left you all here, you know. Why don't you quit thinking with your lizard brain for two seconds and work the problem?"

Plus, I'd really like to see Ames' face when I got there long before sunup, and if I was being honest with myself, I'd like to see Acosta's, too. A teensy part of me wanted to know if he'd be proud that I made it back on time.

Ugh. Get it together, Wren. He is not going to give two shits whether you make it back or not, nor will he wave a banner in the air if you get everyone back safely.

But that didn't mean that wasn't exactly what I wanted to do.

The class was getting restless, and if I didn't cough up some water soon, I was undoubtedly going to get shanked.

"Look," I grumbled, setting down my ruck, "you can give me your canteen and I can get everyone some water, or you can walk by yourself down the mountain without so much as an idea of where you're going. Those are your options. Take it or leave it."

"And if you start getting cute," Malia hissed, tossing a softball-sized rock in her hand, "I'll cave your stupid little skull in. Got me?"

Note to self: do not piss off Malia.

Purple-hair Guy and Jerk Face raised their hands in surrender.

"Okay, someone get some deadfall for a fire. We

need light to see this damn map," I suggested, glad I had at least a few people on my side. Jerk Face took off into the trees, hopefully going to collect some sticks big enough for a torch or something.

One by one everyone passed their canteens to me, and I distributed the water while Purple-hair Guy started a fire. Granted, he tried starting it with his magic first, but failed. When we had a bit of light, I pulled the laminated map from the bag, along with the compass, and a few other items from the dark recesses.

Unfortunately, other than far too many dive weights, there wasn't much more than what looked like water purifying drops and a pocketknife. Good to know if we found water, I could at least make it drinkable—in theory.

Unfolding the map, I tried to gauge where we were. Sure, I'd been camping roughly a zillion times with Ellie and her family, but I'd never been dropped out in the middle of nowhere and told to find my way back. My orienteering skills weren't exactly on point. Most witches knew the directions just by breathing. I didn't have that luxury, my wonky magic fucking even that up.

I latched onto the compass, trying to decipher the map.

"No," Fiona breathed, staring at the slick map, her eyes

widening before narrowing to slits. "They did not have us march in fucking circles all damn day." She pointed at a spot on the paper, looked around, and then pointed at a spot very close to her other finger. "We're here," she said, her eyes lighting up with relief. "See that dip? It matches the terrain over there. Our camp is maybe a mile away."

An all-day hike only to go in circles? Yeah, that sounded about right.

But the sneaky part was that if we hadn't had that map, we'd be wandering in the woods until we *maybe* stumbled on the camp.

"Who wants to show these instructors they can't break us?" I asked, my grin just a touch evil. If Margot Bannister couldn't break me, I seriously doubted the ABI would be able to do the job.

Forty-five minutes later the camp finally came into view, cabin three's pitched roof never looking so good. Granted, I hadn't really inspected it before now, but damn, was it pretty.

In the back of my mind, I was already eating a fair-style turkey leg while I took the longest, hottest shower in the known universe. Though, as soon as the roofline registered to some people, they raced for the cabins like their life depended on it. I was at the back, Fiona's arm slung over my shoulder as she hobbled with renewed vigor. She'd turned her ankle a while back, the darkness most definitely not on her side.

It was clearly well before sunup, and since there was nary an instructor to greet us, I figured no one expected us to get back this fast. Relief hit me as soon as Fiona and I stepped onto the packed dirt of the camp, the flat terrain a blessing after trying not to fall down a hill for so long.

"Well, well, well," Ames called from somewhere, sending my gaze skittering around to try and locate him. "It figures *you'd* be the one to disobey orders."

But we hadn't been given an order not to help—not really.

He separated himself from the shadows as he stalked over to us. This wasn't a man who seemed to be in charge of his mental faculties. Ducking under Fiona's arm, I moved in front of her. For some reason, she seemed to need more protecting than I did.

"You want to tell me why you disobeyed a direct order, cadet?" he snarled, looming over me, even though he was only a handful of inches taller. "You were told not to help your classmates."

Was I really going to get in trouble for doing the right thing? It looked like it.

"Technically," I began, making his rage-filled eyes widen, "there was no order. Commandant Girard said helping would earn punishment—not that we couldn't do it. I'm the one who helped after we were dropped in an unfamiliar terrain in the dark without supplies. If making sure everyone made it back safe and sound is a crime, you can go right ahead and punish me."

Was I daring a man who seemed to have no qualms about accosting someone he was supposed to teach? Maybe. But he wasn't getting the girl at my back.

No way, no how.

Ames' eyes narrowed, his shoulders bunching like he'd really enjoy punching me in the face, but a slow clap had his expression clearing in an instant. He took a step back, grinding his teeth as he straightened, his eyes promising vengeance.

A deep male laugh had shivers racing up my spine—the good kind this time. "Give it a rest, Ames. She beat us at our own game."

Turning the both of us to keep Fiona away from Ames, I spied Acosta stalking from the tree line behind us.

So I guess we were never really alone out there.

Oops?

"Hit the showers and then grab some grub," Acosta ordered, making everyone snap to. "Cadet Bannister here has just volunteered to put every cabin to rights so you all can get a good night's rest. We're starting early tomorrow, ladies and gentlemen, so get to it."

My stomach yowled in protest. I wanted a shower and food. But most of all I wanted sleep.

"Oh, no," Fiona whispered, her whole body trembling as Ames' gaze narrowed on the other instructor. She audibly gulped, and then she backed me up. "I helped, too. No one else could read the map. She shouldn't have to do it alone."

My lips pressed together so I wouldn't start bawling. Fiona could barely stand up on her own, and she wanted to help?

"Me too," the purple-haired guy—AKA, Benjamin—protested. "I gathered sticks for torches and helped people across streams."

"And me," Hannah called. "I provided security and passed out water. We all helped each other. Punishing only her is wrong."

Acosta's smile was feral and yet somehow warm. "Yes, but she was your leader. I watched every step you all made out there. Not a one of you would have made it back without her. I'd have been scooping you all up and shipping you back to your mommies."

As good as the praise felt, my stomach was still mad at me. If only those damn rucks had food in them.

"Get what you need for your showers and get some

food," Acosta ordered, but no one moved, a solid mutiny working its way through the crowd.

"Now," he growled, that single word laced with enough power to make me want to kneel. Hell, if I weren't holding Fiona up, I probably would have.

Everyone moved—even Fiona—her pitiful hobble away making my heart lurch. Her ankle was the size of a grapefruit and most likely broken.

"Jacobs, go to the medic first. Dumond, you take her."

"On it," Hannah muttered, scooping up Fiona like she weighed nothing.

His gaze moved to me, the first time he'd looked directly at me since Ames had thrown his hissy fit—what felt like a week ago—before sliding right off to stare at the instructor in question. "I've got this, Ames. You can clock off, yeah?"

The asshole shook himself like he had no idea he was still standing there. He shot me a scathing glare before marching off as if he'd been the one to suggest it. I sort of wished I knew what his problem was, but it warred with the smart part of my brain that knew it was not my business.

If I had a guess, the name Bannister was the likely culprit.

Two decades ago, the Bannister name heralded a

rich ancestry of powerful witches, deep pockets, and a boatload of influence. Today, my lovely fuckups tarnished our name so bad it was a wonder I made it here in the first place. Someone somewhere had to have pulled quite a few strings to keep me out of jail—something I was lamenting hardily at that particular moment.

At least in jail I wouldn't have to worry about sepsis from a muddy blister on my heel.

My gaze tracked Ames as he stomped off, his form blending into the darkness as soon as he moved out of the dim light amassed from the cabin porch lanterns.

"You did good out there," Acosta murmured, pulling my gaze back to him. I was so tired, I'd almost forgotten I was standing there covered in sweat, dirt, and blood. Wiggling a toe, I nodded.

Yup, definitely bleeding.

"It was no big deal. I'm sure someone else would have done the same if they'd saved their pack." Or I was being incredibly naïve. That was a failing of mine. It was hard for me to think of only the worst in people. Maybe if I had thought about myself a little bit, I wouldn't be stuck here now.

He shifted, moving closer to me, and I had the very sudden realization that we were alone out here. "I don't hand out compliments, Wren. You acted like a leader out there because you are one. But that's going to paint a target on your back just as much as your name will."

The sound of him saying my name had my knees knocking together. Did he say something after that? Oh, that's right, I was in deep shit. Yeah, I knew that already.

"For giving a shit that people didn't fall off this bull- shit mountain and die? I *guess.*" I tried to shrug my shoulders, but every muscle felt like it was going to snap in half and slither off my body. "I was raised better than that."

Acosta snorted, the derision on his face curling his upper lip. "By Margot Bannister? Unlikely."

My gaze narrowed, my jaw clenching. What the hell did he know about my mother?

"Margot Bannister is a name on a birth certificate. Alice Whitlock raised me, and she taught me better than only looking out for myself. That a prize is nothing if I have to sacrifice my honor to get it." I met his gold gaze, those eyes for once not making me melt. "Letting people fall off a cliff because I wanted to win? That would be losing my honor. If that means I have to clean up wall lockers, well, then, so be it."

Pivoting on a heel, I tried to stalk off, but my poor feet had other plans. My stalk was more of a limp, the pitiful squish of my boot making my exit less than ideal.

Plus, a warm hand caught my elbow, the gentle hold sending shivers down my spine.

"You know damn well everyone is trying to clean up their areas before you can get to them," he murmured, his breath close to my ear. The heat of his hand on my skin had my knees ready to give out. "You impressed them all out there. This was a task they were meant to fail, and they know it."

My eyes stayed glued to his hand on my arm. I wanted to look up into those eyes, but if I did, I knew I'd do something stupid. Like faint or kiss him or...

"Look at me," he growled, yanking my gaze up like all I needed was the order. His nostrils flared as his eyes narrowed, almost like he was mad at me for something —the change in his demeanor quick enough to give me whiplash. Leaning in closer, he growled, "You're bleeding. How long have you been bleeding, Wren?"

Why did my name on his lips make my insides go funny? But the best I could do was shrug.

Again.

"I was too scared to look. I worried if I took the boot off to check, I wouldn't be able to get it back on. Walking in the middle of nowhere without shoes on seemed like a bad plan."

Gently, I tugged on my arm, signaling him to let me

go, but all it did was make his eyes start glowing as a growl rumbled from his chest.

No moving. Got it.

"You need a fucking keeper, you know that?" he murmured, the words harsh but his tone was something else. He readjusted his grip, pulling me closer, his nose barely an inch from mine as his gaze bore a hole into me. "When are you going to start looking out for yourself, huh?"

My wolf wouldn't let me do it another second.

Without a word, I lifted the pack off her shoulders, the slight weight probably too much for her to carry that long. An angry red indention bloomed across her pale skin under her soiled tank top, making my eye twitch and my teeth grind.

The pragmatic part of my brain argued once again that she wasn't my mate, but my wolf stomped it down and told it to shut the fuck up. Either mate or spell or blind baser need, Wren needed to be taken care of, and I didn't trust her to do it herself.

In an instant, I had her pack on my shoulder and her lithe body in my arms, her scent powering through the dirt and grime and sweat of the last twenty-four hours. Ignoring her frightened squeak, I marched us toward the only place I wanted her to be.

"Where are you ta—"

"Hush," I barked, refusing to look at the woman. Looking down at that face would do me in. I was already half-insane. I didn't need one more temptation —not when I needed to see where she was bleeding and stop it. Not when I had to make sure she was okay.

Not stopping for a second, I kicked in the door of my cabin with about as much finesse as a battering ram. The instructors had private quarters, and I'd taken over Wyatt's cabin for this class. My wolf practically yipped

CHAPTER 7

NICO

The scent of her blood had my wolf howling inside my brain, cutting off any and all thought or reason. She was hurt—hurt because I couldn't protect her. Failure threatened to cave in my chest as her green-gold eyes widened at my question.

My failure.

It was true: Wren did need a keeper, and she sure as shit needed to think about herself for a change—no part of my words had been a lie. But they failed to convey just how fucking proud of her I was. No magic to be had, no food, no sleep, and she'd made it so every single one of those ungrateful fuckers made it back to camp.

It took everything I had in me to let her walk that long, to let her starve. And now she was bleeding?

inside my head, the idea that she was in my den, in my space, calming him and riling him up all in one go.

At least I had enough brain power to close the door behind us so no one else could see me completely unravel—except Wren. Her gaze hadn't left my face once, the burn of it racing down my spine all the way to my cock.

Fuck.

Continuing my trek, I strode to the private bath. Unlike the cadets, each instructor had a studio-style cabin outfitted with a full bath, kitchenette, microscopic living room, and bedroom. They were small and bare bones, but it got the job done. I didn't see any of it, my eyes on the prize of getting those damn boots of hers off so I could inspect her feet.

You could have gone to the medic instead. Why did you bring her here?

I knew the answer to that question, but avoided it like the plague, my wolf slashing his claws into my brain.

Reluctantly, I set Wren down on the closed toilet lid and flipped on the shower tap. She had been rucking through mud and dirt and who knew what else—she'd need to get cleaned up before I could dress her feet. Yes, that was the very good reason I had for stealing her away to my cabin without so much as a word.

Yep.

Totally logical.

"Umm... A-Acosta? I don—"

The sound of my last name passing her lips grated, making my jaw clench. "Nico," I growled, kneeling at her feet. "My name is Nico."

Eyes wide, she blinked at me as she digested the situation. "O-okay, Nico. I don't know what's going on, and I'd really like to."

While fair, I couldn't exactly give her an answer. I didn't know what was going on, either. "You're bleeding and covered in filth and about as sturdy as a cooked noodle."

All true, but not what she'd asked. Too bad, it was all I could give her.

Without further explanation, my gaze reluctantly left her face as I focused on the laces of her boots crusted with dried mud. Gently, I pulled one loose, working the lace so it was wide enough that I could pull her foot free.

As soon as I pulled on the ruined leather, she hissed and pressed a hand to her mouth as her face drained of all color. With nothing else for it, I yanked her foot free of the boot, barely managing to catch her before she went limp, passing out from shock or pain or worse. I didn't bother to look at her freed foot. Instead, I worked the other boot off while she was still passed out.

When I finally let myself move my gaze down, though, both my wolf and I nearly howled. Wren's feet were hamburger—blistered and swollen, completely covered in blood. Her socks were soaked, ripped in some places as the material had been worn thin by the sheer amount of walking. I'd never wanted to wring someone's neck as much as I did this woman's.

Why hadn't she said anything? Why didn't she tell me she was hurt?

She doesn't know you, stupid. And did you see every other instructor out there? Those kids would have been put through the wringer.

Cradling her to my chest, I tried to calm down as I waited, burying my nose in her hair in an attempt to appease my wolf. He wouldn't be satisfied until she was healed, until she was mine, until she was underneath me. But I could only help with one of those.

My eyes slid closed as I used the lone ability not given to me by my father.

The one I never used unless it was absolutely necessary.

The one I would not hesitate to use now.

Reaching inside the deepest parts of me, I called for my wolf, pulling at the thread of him until he reached back. I drew from him—drew on the healing that he so often gave to me, and clutched Wren closer, passing on that power.

Not all Alphas could perform this healing, the ability lost over the centuries as brute force and subjugation became far more revered.

It was as if I were a conduit, letting the energy flow from me to her in a steady pulse of heat, quietly drawing her pain away. I gritted my teeth against it, the sharp ache of the process leaving me cold and shaky.

How was she standing with pain like that? How was she breathing?

Pulling more from her, I sucked in a gasp. Her joints were on fire, her back aching, and her clawing hunger all slapped me at once, turning my stomach. But I could shoulder it. If it meant she wouldn't hurt anymore, if it meant my wolf would be soothed, if it meant this terrible throb in my chest would go away, I'd do it.

The heat of the water misted through the room as her scent filled my nose, and I slid my eyes open, inspecting her feet.

The damage was still substantial, but she wasn't actively bleeding anymore, nor did the flesh seem to be one wrong move away from infection. A tiny bit of pride suffused my chest, quelling that stupid ache I'd felt since the day I pulled her from the flames. It was always there, nagging, gnawing, picking at me until I saw her, until I scented her, until I held her.

Wren seemed to startle in my arms, yanking herself to consciousness by sheer force of will. Shuddering, she reached for her feet, even as my arms held her tight. Mesmerized, her hand shook as she gently prodded the wounds, her body stilling at the same moment her fingers did.

"How did you... You hea—"

"I didn't *do* anything," I lied through my teeth. For some reason, having her know was so much worse than her thinking she'd healed on her own. I had no idea why she shouldn't, I just knew it was bad.

No one but my mother knew what I could do— knew about the quiet alpha power that so few used.

And I didn't trust Wren.

Wanting her didn't equate to trust in my book.

"You should get cleaned up," I croaked, though I hoped it passed muster as a rumble.

Images of her stripping off her clothes filled my brain. Of the water sliding down her creamy skin. Of her flesh pebbling at the kiss of the water.

Nope. I needed to stop that thought right in its tracks.

But her scent in my nose, coupled with her short little pants, and the gallop of her heart were calling to every single instinct I had. My wolf howled, begging me to bury my face in her neck and take that scent for our own.

To make it ours.

"I'll leave you to it," I murmured, pulling us both up. I had to get out of this room before I looked at her face. One look and I would be done for.

Setting her away from me, I made for the door, only to be jerked to a stop by her voice.

"What do I do for clothes?" That voice was deep and husky and affected, and I desperately tried to ignore how her scent had changed.

Don't look. Do not look at her. You won't make it out of this room.

"I'll take care of it," I murmured, slipping out of the confined space before my wolf decided to do something stupid.

But as soon as the door closed behind me, a new dilemma dawned. The only clothes in this cabin were mine. Dancing in my head were the images of my shirt sliding over her shower-warmed skin. Of her bare ass barely hidden by the hem. Of her rosy nipples pebbling against the cotton. My name written across her back as my fingers fisted in her hair.

Nope. No. She needed her own clothes, and I needed to get the hell out of here.

Racing for the door, I breathed a shuddered sigh of relief once the fresh night air hit my nostrils, her scent diluted by the perfume of pine trees and fresh earth. Even under sweat and dirt and blood, her scent made me fucking crazy.

I kept to the shadows, picking through the camp as I made a beeline for her cabin.

She needed her own clothes. Her. Own. Clothes.

With a cursory check to make sure no one was inside, I followed that honey and jasmine scent to her bunk, dispassionately selecting underwear and soft garments to make sure she was comfortable, remembering the flip-flops by chance.

There was no way she would be able to put those boots on again without pain—it didn't matter how much of the sting I'd been able to leech from her.

A few moments later, I was back at my cabin, desperately trying to quiet my wolf. He was so loud, I didn't even hear the water shut off. I'd had every intention of simply setting them on the toilet, but before I could, she opened the bathroom door.

Wrapped in the luckiest towel known to mankind, she stuttered to a stop as clouds of steam carrying her intoxicating scent surrounded me. Her warm, wet skin pebbled against the cool air just like I feared it would, the heat of it reaching me.

One pull and that towel could be gone.

One step and she'd be in my arms.

One kiss and she'd be in my bed.

Fuck.

I was doomed.

CHAPTER 8
WREN

Was this what prey felt like?

Nico's golden eyes glowed with whatever power he kept hidden beneath his flesh. I wasn't quite certain what class of arcaner he was, but whatever it may have been, I was pretty sure it was some sort of predator.

His jaw clenched as he stared at me, the wadded bundle of fabric in his arms forgotten. Yes, I was acutely aware I was in a towel, still damp from the most blessed shower I had ever taken. Sure, the water pressure left something to be desired, but there was soap and shampoo and even a conditioner that smelled like Heaven.

But the crux of it was that I didn't have a stitch on

me, and he did—specifically, he had what appeared to be my clothes in his hands.

"Are those for me?" I squeaked, my voice—along with my belly—doing very weird things at the moment. I couldn't feel my feet and the aches in my bones were long gone. And the way he was staring at me, like he'd really enjoy eating me up, well...

Nico took three long steps toward me, his gaze never leaving my face. He didn't say a word as his jaw clenched and unclenched, like any second, he'd stop holding himself back and kiss me or devour me or...

My whole body vibrated with the growing silence, or maybe that was Nico's growl. He seemed almost frozen, my near nakedness shorting out the rational part of his brain.

Hell, I was having a tough time not just reaching up and giving this little towel a tug. I didn't know the first thing about him, and the reckless section of my head didn't seem to give a shit.

My foot moved forward, not bothering to consult the rest of my mind, but as soon as my skin made contact with the floor, the pain came roaring back, making me wince. A hiss escaped my lips and that small sound seemed to break us both out of our haze.

"Here," he growled, handing me the bundle in his arms. "Get dressed, and I'll bandage your feet."

I was barely able to nod before he gently pushed me back in the bathroom and shut the door, the slap of the wood making contact with the frame the bucket of cold water I needed.

He's your instructor, Wren. You have enough problems trying to survive this stupid school without fucking your instructor on the second damn day.

As usual, my inner voice was right. A hint of shame made my heart ache as I hurriedly slipped into my clothes—or as hurried as one could be while trying not to aggravate their cut-up feet. He'd brought me a comfortable bra and underwear, a pair of lounge shorts, and a soft, oversized T-shirt that I frequently slept in.

That ache in my chest? Well, it doubled as his kindness hit me. He could have left me there or sent me to the medic.

Then why didn't he?

I didn't have an answer to that, and I doubted he did, either.

Without the desire to ransack Nico's bathroom for a brush, I messily piled my wet hair on top of my head and opened the door. Nico was in the small kitchen, bracing his hands against the counter as he hung his head.

"Everything okay?" I murmured, unwilling to step farther into the room. It wasn't the pain in my feet, either. There seemed to be a weight in the air between us in that unknown space that resided there.

"Fine."

Nico shoved back from the counter and strode over to me. Without a word, he lifted me up in his arms, carrying me to the kitchen. His scent enveloped me, the woodsy wild cologne surrounding me. He'd been out in those woods all damn day, and yet, he smelled like I wanted to lick his neck and reach my hand down his pants.

Where the fuck did that come from? Get it together, Wren.

The cool kiss of the counter against my ass had me shaking myself. My feet were still injured—not as much as before, I knew that much. Nico had to have done something, worked some kind of magic on me. But how?

Maybe it was the wards that protected us, maybe it was just him, but no one had ever been able to use magic around me without consequences.

Ever.

So how was he able to help me?

His hands left my skin, and he studiously ignored me while he readied his supplies, opening a jar of salve with a jerking twist.

Wincing, I stayed his hand before he could grab my

foot. I'd have to warn him, and I really didn't want to. "That stuff is spell-free, right?"

Frowning, he jerked his gaze to mine. "Why?"

Screwing my mouth to the side, his shoulders hunched all on their own. "Magic goes wonky around me. Spells? They go haywire."

Nico's face blanked, shuttering completely before I could figure out what he was thinking. Not that I knew —ever—but before I could sort of guess.

Now his face was a mask of nothing, like maybe he didn't believe me and didn't want me to know it.

The tried-and-true sense of shame crawled out of its hidey-hole to slap me in the face. I couldn't expect him to understand something like that. The Bannisters were one of the oldest witch families in the States. We had been a legacy once upon a time.

Now because of me, we were a joke.

Or *I* was.

Dropping my gaze, I inspected the floor, counting rows of hardwood planks rather than looking him in the eye anymore.

This was stupid. I was stupid. I never should have come here. They should have just sent me to prison and threw away the key. At least there I couldn't hurt anyone. At least there I could be where I belonged with all the other fuckups.

"Yes, it's free of magic," he murmured. "It's a regular salve for cuts and bruises. May I?"

Jerkily, I nodded, not bothering to look at him. His fingers found my ankle and he held my leg steady while he gently spread the ointment over the worst of the cuts.

Other witches could heal themselves up just fine. Me? I was stuck with human-grade healing and no way to speed up the process. Under the null wards, at least the rest of my class was in the same boat. Part of me wished for a way to synthesize those wards down to something smaller so I could walk down the street in peace.

It didn't have to be in Savannah, either.

I'd like to go anywhere where the Bannister name wasn't known. I'd like to go into a shop without worrying I would hurt someone. Or maybe simply live in the knowledge that my bullshit existence—such as it was—wasn't a blight on the butt of humanity.

Gritting my teeth against the sting of the ointment, I started counting the planks on the walls, avoiding the man who was so carefully tending to my wounds.

How do you keep getting into situations like this? Can't you keep your nose clean for one day, Wren?

My inner voice was sounding an awful lot like my mother these days.

In no time at all, Nico was done with the salve and on to wrapping my battered feet in gauze. I wasn't sure how I was supposed to keep them clean and dry in an environment like this. If the coming weeks were anything like the last twenty-four hours, I was screwed.

I'd likely end up with gangrene and die. Wouldn't that just be a cherry on top of the shit sundae that was this week?

When he started taping the gauze down, I'd formulated a likely flawed plan. I could go to the kitchens and maybe pilfer their plastic baggie supply. That would at least keep mud and dirt out of my wounds—in theory.

I was in the middle of my baggie heist plans when Nico moved in my space, his face right in mine.

"You're going to take care of yourself, right?" It was less a question and more of a direct order.

The best I could do was shrug. Did it really matter? If I washed out, I'd go to jail where I'd always planned on going, anyway. What did it matter if I washed out medically or because of outright failure? Either way, I would still be the family fuckup.

"If another all-day hike is on the menu, I might fail on purpose. Jail is sounding better and better all the time."

His gold eyes started glowing again as his hands

bracketed my hips on the counter. His body seemed to get bigger, wider, as he loomed over me.

"You do realize that jail is off the table for you, right? If you wash out of this course, jail isn't your fallback. Execution is."

A cold pit of dread yawned wide in my belly.

"But... it wasn't even my fault! I told him to stop. That he couldn't do the spell around me." Yes, I'd just admitted to bribing a warlock to do a spell for me in the first place, but the punishment for that wasn't *death*. Hell, neither was burning his shop down.

The punishment according to the witch covenant was reparations and jail time. Not...

"They don't care, Wren," he murmured, his warm breath skating over my skin. "You need to get your shit together. You need to succeed here. Because there is no fallback plan for you."

Gulping hard, the dread snaked its fingers through my entire chest, making the breaths in my lungs stutter. No fallback plan. No jail. No safety net.

I gritted my teeth against the urge to curl up into a ball and start screaming. This wasn't fair—none of it.

"Deep breaths," he commanded, cupping my chin in his hands. "Breathe in for the count of four and out for four."

When I didn't comply immediately, he tilted my chin up almost roughly, getting my attention.

"Breathe, Wren. In for four and out for four. Do it."

With nothing else for it, I did what he said, sucking in breaths as he counted. Still shaking, my breathing regulated.

"Good girl. Now what are you going to do?"

"Pass. Survive," I croaked, and a hint of a smile lifted the side of his mouth.

He took a short step closer, his slim hips fitting in between my knees. "Good. And you're going to take care of yourself, right?"

His scent enveloped me in a tight embrace, and even though he wasn't touching me anymore, I still felt him everywhere. My heart picked up speed once again, only this time it wasn't the threat of death or the pain.

It was him so close to me, his scent in my nose, and his mouth so close to mine. I wanted to fall into that mouth, lose myself for a second in those lips. Hypnotized, my torso drifted closer to his, my breasts brushing the wall of his chest.

I nodded in answer, brushing my nose against his with the movement. All I could see were his glowing gold eyes, as the rumble of a growl vibrated through us both. The heat in them made those eyes pools of molten metal as his lids drooped just a touch.

A shuddering gasp squeezed from my throat in anticipation, the almost-touch too much for me to bear.

And then all I felt was cool air as Nico's gaze narrowed to slits and he moved back.

"You should get some sleep," he practically growled, half-turning his body away from me.

Confused, the cold slap of rejection woke me from my trance.

Oh. *Oh*. I was so stupid. I'd misread him somewhere. He didn't...

Swallowing thickly, I gingerly hopped off the counter, gritting my teeth against the pain in my chest and the ache in my feet.

"Thanks for..." *Everything?* "Your help and advice. I appreciate it."

How I'd strung those words together without bawling was a fucking miracle, but I did it. I didn't meet his gaze the entire time, but I fucking did it.

And I could do this. I could make it back to my bunk and... and...

Stupid tears welled in my eyes as I looked for the flip-flops Nico had brought with him in my bundle of clothes. I'd left them in the other room, along with my filthy clothes and ruined boots. Clenching my teeth against the pain, I minced to the bathroom and snatched everything up, sliding my poor feet into the scant shoes.

He'd been so kind and all I'd taken it as was a plea to fuck me. Gods, I was so fucking dumb.

I made a move to go out the front door, when he caught me by the arm. "It's not safe to go that way," he murmured, the sound of his voice making me want to crawl in a hole and just... "You need to use the back door."

Wetly, I chuckled, the shame and mirth of the double entendre warring in my chest. It wasn't the first time I'd been shoved out the back door so no one would see. And even though I had the mental maturity of a twelve-year-old boy, everything just hurt.

It *hurt.*

Pulling my arm from his grip, I let him lead me to the door that was hidden in a back nook of the cabin. I could do this. I could walk back to my cabin and shore myself up and pass this gods-forsaken course.

I could.

It didn't matter that my mother thought I was the worst mistake she'd ever made or that my grandmother wished I'd have never been born. I could be a halfway decent agent if I put my mind to it, right?

Maybe be an analyst or a researcher. No one in their

right mind would let me out in the field, but I could be useful. I could matter.

Steeling my spine, I marched out the door, not looking back at Nico. He'd helped me, healed me, and patched me up. He could have my thanks and that was it.

My march turned into a hobble after about a minute, the trek to the cadet cabins far longer than Nico had made it seem. By the time I made it to the porch, I was breathing funny, sweating, and so close to tears it was dumb. All I had to do was make sure the cabin was clean and I could go get some food.

My stomach howled in agreement. Food would make it better.

But before I could close my fingers around the handle, it was yanked out of my grip. Fiona stood in the open doorway, a relieved smile on her face. She was clean, walking on her own two feet, and seemed a lot better than when I'd left her. It made me wonder just how long I'd been gone.

"Get in here," she insisted, looping an arm around my middle, and helping me to my bunk. The cabin itself was also clean, Hannah's bed righted and made, and Malia's locker back to order.

Fiona was chittering about how the other cabins had cleaned up their own messes and how no one was going to let me lift a finger. A warmth built up under my ribs, easing the ache there a bit.

"Thanks," I whispered, squeezing her hand as she settled in next to me on my bed. "I really appreciate you guys."

She snorted, shaking her head. "You know damn well we would have all fallen off this damn rock without you. Even if no one else says it, you saved us. For some of us, the ABI is all we have left. It's our last option. I won't forget how you helped me, Wren. Not ever."

That was it. I was going to start crying any second now.

"Quit it before I start sobbing into my pillow," I grumbled, gently shoving her shoulder. "How's your ankle?"

She lifted the formerly offending appendage in the air to show me. "Good as new. The healer here is fabulous, plus it's the one place where the null wards aren't —except for the practical areas—so I got to actually breathe. I swear, these wards are for the birds."

The reality of what could have happened if I would have taken her to the healer sobered me. Gods, would there ever be a time where I could just be normal? Ever?

The cabin door opened, Hannah and Malia filing in, both their arms loaded down with plates.

"Look who's back," Hannah said, a wide smile

blooming over her face as a knowing look filled her eyes. I didn't quite know what that was about, but I had a feeling I didn't *want* to know. "We picked you up some grub."

"More like she bribed the cook to heat up everything he could before she threatened to eat him, but whatever," Malia teased, a sly smile curling her lips.

"I didn't say I was going to eat him," Hannah protested. "I said I was hungry and growled a little, that's all. It's his fault if he assumed."

Hannah had informed us that ghouls only had to eat flesh every six months or so to stay healthy, and more often than not, they chose the freshly dead to consume. Most were morgue attendants or funeral home directors —fitting into polite society with ease.

She dropped a plate on my lap and handed me a fork. "Eat up. Tomorrow is going to be a doozy, and that Ames fucker has a bug up his ass about you."

I took the fork, and it was as if it unlocked my hunger. A moment later, I was drowning my sorrows in mashed potatoes. I'd eat, and sleep, and tomorrow I wouldn't look at Nico—*Acosta*—once.

And I'd make it.

Wouldn't I?

CHAPTER 9
NICO

F our.
　　　Fucking.
　　　Days.

That's how long it had been since Wren looked in my direction. Four days since I watched those green-gold eyes spark with heat, since I let her scent wrap around me like I was sinking into her body. Four days since she acknowledged me at all.

Four days since I fucked up.

But what else was I supposed to do? I had already been pushing it taking her back to my cabin—a solid idiot move, if I do say so myself. If I'd have kissed her, there would have been no stopping us. I would have fucked her right on that tiny kitchen counter, and then where would she be?

My bed.

Where would I?

My bed.

Because I sure as shit wouldn't be letting her out of it once I had her, that much was certain. The way she called to the wolf under my flesh made every single minute of the last four days its own version of hell on earth.

I didn't know if I believed her tale of not being able to do magic. Or that she hadn't set fire to Carmichael's shop. If she couldn't do magic like she said, then why the fuck was I so damn smitten with her? Why did my eyes follow her every movement?

Why did I still feel the heat of her body against mine four days later?

Gritting my teeth, I watched her grip the rifle with the moderate efficiency of someone who had handled a gun a time or two. She wasn't failing, but she wasn't a sharp-shooter either, which was exactly where I wanted her to be.

She needed to keep her head down. She needed to survive.

But even though she hadn't looked at me once, she still did exactly what I'd told her to. So far, she'd passed every test, no matter how much Ames threw at her. But there was a cold look of determination behind her eyes that I hated—mostly because I'd been the one to put it there.

That coldness hurt, and it was all my fault.

"Get your shots on target, Bannister, or I'll take that rifle away and give you a fucking BB gun," Ames screamed six inches away from her ear.

I had to give it to him: he hadn't once touched another student since I "counseled" him on his methods, but that didn't stop him from singling Wren out. Unfortunately, there was only so much I could protect her from without waving a huge red flag that I was showing her favor.

My gaze shifted to her target. Out of the twenty shots she'd fired, she'd hit about fifteen center mass and four in the head. The lone shot she'd missed, was barely a centimeter off. And what was worse? The poor bastard next to Wren hadn't managed to hit the target more than a handful of times.

Wren's cheeks pinked as her eyes narrowed, not sparing Ames a glance. In quick succession, she fired off six shots, each one hitting the target right in the head. I had a feeling she'd been picturing Ames' face while she did it, too.

Then again, it could have been mine.

The scent of her sorrow was still in my nose, the

rejection and sudden change in my attitude undoing every good thing I'd done since taking her to my stupid cabin. I'd hurt her. A lot.

"I guess I just need to yell at you every time you shoot, then, now, don't I? I mean how else are we going to get you ready for the real ABI?"

Gods, Ames was such a fucking idiot.

The instructor straightened, narrowing his eyes at me. Out of the two of us, my students were actually being taught by a competent instructor and doing fine. His eight students—save for Wren and a few others—were floundering.

Barnes was barely hitting the target, Faust was still trying to load his rifle after twenty minutes, and Ponda's weapon was in pieces on his lap.

Raising an eyebrow at him, I circled my finger, signaling for him to wrap it the fuck up. We needed to move this along and him not helping the others wasn't going to get us all to lunch on time. Ames' hands fisted at his sides, his anger getting the best of him as he stalked over.

"What?" he hissed, glaring at me. "You mad because I'm schooling your girl?"

And this was exactly what I'd been afraid of when he walked up to me that night before the course officially began. The last thing I needed was him figuring out just how much Wren meant to me. Irritated, I crooked my finger, walking back a few paces out of the null line where I knew no one could hear us.

"No, I'm mad, because despite the time you've spent 'schooling' a cadet that doesn't need it, Ponda's weapon has come apart, and Faust hasn't got a shot off. You have eight students. Not one. I cannot teach all sixteen by myself or... maybe I can, and you should go take a nap since you're acting like a fucking toddler."

But then I'd have to get closer to Wren, and I had a feeling she'd like to turn that gun on me.

"What do you mean?" Ames whipped his head to stare at the wonder twins who were fucking up royally. "Oh, for fuck's sake. Gods, those two are going to give me a fucking aneurysm. If it isn't arcane related, they act like it doesn't fucking exist."

Ames marched right back to the wonder twins and started his rant while I got Barnes in hand, putting me right next to Wren.

Fuck.

Her scent filled my nose again, and it was as if my wolf had been waiting for it. He whined in my head, begging me to get closer. But I'd been dealing with his complaints for four fucking days, so gritting my teeth against them was nothing new.

By the time Ames was done kicking Faust and Ponda off the range, I'd managed to get my wolf under control and fix the problem with Barnes' sights that had him aiming for the fucking moon.

Ames pressed the red range button that signaled everyone to put their weapons down. "Police your brass and stow your weapons. It's time to finally get to the fun part of this exercise."

Ames slapped the blue button, recalling the targets and replacing them with closer ones. He opened the closest locker, revealing rows upon rows of glowing orbs.

Wren stumbled back, trying to get as far away from Ames as she possibly could without drawing attention to herself. Her fiery braid practically trembled against her back as she seemed to search for an exit. Ames called a few cadets up to pass out the potion bombs, but I was more focused on Wren's face going white.

She was typically pale, but red splotches were forming on her chest as her breathing hitched in her throat. Wide-eyed, her panic permeated the air as she shuffled back. I'd figured she'd been lying to me when she said she couldn't do magic, but what had she said?

Magic goes wonky around me. Spells? They go haywire.

I didn't know how much of that was true. Sure, it seemed like it was true with her freaking out, but—

Wren's scared steps had her accidentally knocking into Barnes who had a blue orb in his hands. Barnes, the clumsy idiot with a shock of purple hair, fumbled the orb before dropping it. Wren dove for it, managing to catch the orb before it broke, her face white as a sheet.

Hell, she looked like she was ready to throw up.

Gently, she handed it back to Barnes before steeling her spine and marching over to Ames.

"Get back to your spot, Bannister," Ames barked, his hands full of potion crates.

Wren shook her head, her knees knocking together, even though her shoulders were back. "I can't," she insisted. "Someone is going to get hurt if I stay here."

Ames rolled his eyes as he passed off a crate to another student. "Yeah, yeah. We all know about your penchant for blowing things up. No one gives a shit. Get in line."

"You don—"

Ames advanced on her. "I said get back in line, or I'll make sure you're booted out of this school so fast it'll make your head spin." A cruel smile bloomed across his mouth. "Literally."

That little fuck. He was taunting her, baiting her.

Threatening her.

I clenched my teeth against my wolf's howl as I watched Wren shrink back.

What are you doing? You're just going to stand there while he threatens her? You aren't worthy of her as a mate, you selfish prick.

But she wasn't my mate, and even if she was, how could I defend her here? In front of all these cadets? No, I'd need something else, something lasting so Ames knew never to fuck with her again. Mate or not, I couldn't watch her all the time, and with this kind of escalation, it was only going to get worse.

"All right, people. Take a single potion bomb and aim for your target," Ames called loudly. "These are light arms, little more than colorful smoke bombs. They are often employed by agents to help clear a room, or based on the spell, incapacitate a perp. Since they are training rounds, they are mostly neutralized except for a tiny bit of magic."

The quickness with which Ames went from threatening Wren's life to following the lesson plan made my stomach turn.

Ames' face twisted into a scowl when Wren made no move to touch the potion crate. "What did I tell you, Bannister? Pick up a potion bomb."

I noticed the instant she was going to defy him and moved, getting right in her space, managing not to stare into those gorgeous eyes by sheer force of will.

"Maybe if Miss Bannister doesn't want to complete

this iteration," I growled threateningly as I latched a hand around her bicep, "she'd be better served cleaning the dining facility." But my will crumbled in an instant, and my gaze found hers, anyway. "Maybe that'll teach you to bail on lessons."

Roughly, I jerked her away from the line as the first potion bomb was thrown. What was supposed to be a little smoke bomb turned into a ball of fire as soon as the glass smashed against the target. Green flames coated the grass beneath, blanketing the ground in an inferno.

Too late to stop the onslaught, the other potion bombs were already in the air, their landings detonating like the bombs they were, and then it wasn't me pulling Wren, it was *her* pulling *me*.

Flames exploded across the berm as the grass caught in an almost-wildfire. All the target stands were engulfed in mere moments as the flames reached farther, almost catching the stands on fire. Students shrieked as they raced for cover, but Wren yanked us toward the null wards, her red braid flying behind her as she dragged us both across it.

Breathing heavily, she stared at the empty firing line, tears pooling in her eyes. As soon as she crossed the line, the flames died, the grass smoldering where the fire had once been.

Shaking, she finally looked at me, something she hadn't done on purpose in four fucking days. Her face was gray as she gulped in air. Eyes wide and shocky, she put a trembling hand to her mouth.

"Did I... did I hurt anyone?" she whispered, a tear cresting her eyelid and falling down her cheek.

Gods, what I wouldn't give to be able to hold her right now. And what I wouldn't give to not have to look away.

But I did, scanning the crowd of students and Ames, trying to scent blood or pain over the pall of smoke and charred grass. I couldn't detect any, and the students seemed to be fine as they dusted themselves off and ventured closer to the stands, their voices buzzing in alarm.

Ames stood, his face white and voice cracking. "Everyone, calm down. Looks like we got the wrong batch from the apothecary. I'll test the next few potions to make sure, but we should be fine."

Wrong batch my ass.

Wren shook her head, the violent motion nearly bringing her to her knees. "They can't," she hissed. "Not while I'm here."

Giving her a quick jerk of my chin, I tightened my hold on her arm and resumed my march toward the dining hall, more to hold her up than anything else, but no one else needed to know that. Plus, I had to keep up the appearance of her "punishment" or Ames might catch on that Wren had most definitely caused that fire.

She'd also caused the Azalea Apothecary blaze, too.

Just not on purpose.

She hadn't been lying to me—she couldn't do magic. Wren couldn't so much as cast a single spell—not without severe consequences. And if she couldn't cast a spell, and all spells around her exploded, she'd never survive here.

They'd toss her out the first chance they got.

My wolf howled, clawing and slashing in my brain hard enough to make me wince. I had to figure something out—if only to give me more time to come to grips with my other realization.

Because if she didn't do magic, then what had she done to me?

"You've never cast a spell?" I asked under my breath —the answer vital if I was going to do this.

If I was going to put my life on the line to... to...

Wren shook her head. "Maybe when I was little, but not since I could remember. I didn't even go to arcane school—too dangerous."

Nodding, I breathed a sigh of relief as the empty dining hall came into view. "And the apothecary?"

"Has everyone heard about that damn thing?" she

asked, her chuckle wet as she shook her head again. "I tried to stop Carmichael and then the whole damn place exploded."

And had I not been there she would have died in those flames.

Fuck, this was a mess.

And all of this meant she hadn't put a spell on me. She didn't make me act this way—at least not on purpose.

And it meant Wren wasn't a fuckup, not really. She had to be cursed or born under the wrong stars or worse. I'd never heard of a witch being born that way. Uninherits, sure, there were plenty of witches who didn't get magic, but to amplify it, to change the magic itself?

No. That was a first.

I couldn't stop the incessant nod or the way my wolf sucked in her scent. It was like she was leaving me, and I needed to keep her in my nose as long as possible.

I had to fix it.

Simply the thought of what could happen if Ames— or anyone—figured out Wren's little magic problem. They'd kill her.

And then I'd kill them.

Ushering her inside the building, I raced for the custodian's closet, dragging her behind me. There, I snatched the bucket and mop, some cleanser, and some rags. It had to look real. It had to look like I was punishing her for not participating, and then...

Then I'd make sure no one knew what she was. No one.

"Stay here and clean the place up. Pout. Make it look good. Lie if you need to. But stay the fuck here, got it?"

Wren stared at me with those gorgeous eyes and didn't say a word. Not until I grabbed her hand and gently shook it.

"A-Acosta—"

"No," I growled, advancing on her until she pressed her back against the wall. "When we're together, when we're alone, you call me Nico. Understand?"

She gulped, tearing her gaze from mine as her shoulders curved in. "No," she croaked. "I don't understand."

Gods, I was a fucking idiot. Hooking a finger under her chin, I lifted her face to mine. Yes, we were in a damn broom closet. Yes, it was the wrong fucking time. Yes, I was being a first-rate asshole, complicating this *whatever* between us, but she needed to look at me.

I *needed* her to look at me. As soon as those gorgeous fucking eyes met mine, I couldn't stop myself from getting closer to her, boxing her in, surrounding her.

"I'm going to fix it," I growled, my voice barely

above a whisper as I lowered my lips to hers. "I'll make it so you're safe here."

It was a promise.

An oath.

A vow.

Her gaze flared as my lips inched closer, and I watched those green-gold embers blaze bright until I was mere millimeters away from Heaven.

"Say my name, Wren," I ordered softly, my lips brushing hers as I spoke. Her breath hitched as her scent rose, her trembling fingers fisting in the fabric of my shirt. "Come on, my beautiful little bird. What's my name?"

"Nico," she breathed—like it was permission and a plea all at the same time.

Putting us both out of our misery, I pressed my lips to hers, sweeping my tongue into her mouth as she parted her lips on a gasp.

Gods.

If she smelled like Heaven, her taste was pure paradise, and the moan that vibrated up her throat? I was a goner with one fucking kiss. Helpless against its pull, I gripped the end of her copper braid and tugged, tilting her head back so I could devour her mouth.

Her scent perfumed the air around us, taking over all my senses as I crushed my mouth to hers. Her tongue stroked mine as her fingers fisted in my hair. Without a moment's hesitation I let go of her braid and found her hips, lifting her up and pressing her further into the wall. The friction of her center against the bulge in my jeans had a groan ripping up my throat.

I wanted her—more than I'd probably wanted anything or anyone else in my whole fucking life.

And I couldn't have her.

Not right now. Not while she wasn't safe.

Just as fiercely as it began, our kiss gentled, our heavy mingled breaths fanning the flames of our need.

Gods, I needed inside her. I needed her creamy skin against my sheets and her moans in my mouth.

"Four days, Wren. I've been wanting to do that for four fucking days."

Her brow furrowed as she took my bottom lip between her teeth, her tongue taunting me as she laved the sting. "Then why didn't you?"

That was a damn good question. "I was trying to keep you safe. I can't keep you safe if I'm distracted."

Her head tilted to the side as if my answer didn't quite make sense. "And I'm distracting?"

Wren's smile was tentative and knowing all at the same time, and I wanted to fuck her against this wall and...

This is not keeping her safe, you idiot. Get your head out of your dick for five seconds, will you?

My hand flexed on her hips as I forced myself to let her down. "You know damn well that you are."

Her expression was just as confused as it had been a moment before, but I couldn't explain—not if I was to get to Savannah and back before nightfall.

Not if I was going to keep her alive.

"Stay here. I'll find you when I get back."

With no time left, I pressed my lips to her forehead as I drew that honey and jasmine perfume into my nose, keeping it for myself. Then I forced myself to let her go, to leave that small piece of Heaven, to walk away from her.

To get in my car and leave her defenseless here while I went to Savannah.

But I needed witch help for a witch problem.

Unfortunately, I'd just have to settle for a warlock.

Too many hours later, my fingers fisted in the filthy fabric of Carmichael Jones' shirt. Knuckles bloody, I drew my arm back once more.

"Either you tell me the truth, or I end you right now, old man. What. Happened?" I growled through clenched teeth. "Don't make me ask again."

Carmichael spat blood on my boot, his eyes lolling in his head. "Fine, okay? I'll tell you. She offered me the money to heal the human, and I started the spell. Then all of a sudden, my whole damn shop is on fire, windows explodin' and everything. I don't know what else you want from me."

It had taken far too long to get this much out of him. I supposed he thought I'd get him in trouble or worse for lying his ass off to the ABI, hence why he was so cagey with the details. "Did she try to get you to stop?"

Carmichael shrugged. "Maybe? She yelled somethin', but then the whole place went up like a dang Roman candle."

"And then you ran off with the money and left her there to die? Is that it?"

"What's it to you?" The old man narrowed his gaze on me, a wide bloody smile on his crooked mouth. "Oh, this is good," he said on a chuckle. "The wolf prince and the Bannister fuckup. You sweet on her, wolf-boy?"

My smile must have been straight out of a nightmare because his fell as fast as mine rose. "And how would that make me any less dangerous to you? If I'm sweet on her like you say, and you left her to die, what's to stop me from ripping your throat out right here and right now?"

Carmichael lifted a shaky hand. "Now, hold on there. Maybe we can work something out. No need to do somethin' rash."

My grin widened. "As a matter of fact, I do think you can help me."

CHAPTER 10
WREN

There was no way that just happened.

No. Way.

Pressing my fingertips against my lips, I stifled a laugh. I'd spent the last four days pretending Nico Acosta didn't exist—the last four days pretending his gentle touches and caring words had meant nothing. That he hadn't destroyed me with a single rejection.

I'd gone over and over it in my head—trying to figure out where I'd gotten it wrong. And now I knew I *hadn't* gotten everything mixed up. He'd wanted me just as much as I'd wanted him.

He just wouldn't let himself have me.

And what did his "I'm going to fix it" mean? I'd been dealing with this horseshit my whole life, and he was going to breeze in and fix it?

How? Was he going to whip out some shells and beads and pray real hard that this curse I'd lived with my entire existence just *went away*?

But a single, solitary section of my brain asked if maybe he *could*.

I'd been cut off from the arcane side of Savannah for more years than I could remember—forever maybe. Even with parents like mine and a grandmother with as much power as she had, no one had even given a passing nod to an attempt at fixing this albatross around my neck.

I *wasn't* a blessed Bannister.

I was a blight. A black spot. A section of decay that they'd rather cut out or forget ever existed than fix whatever it was that had made me this way.

A shining bit of hope broke through the hedge of thorns in my chest—the one that was supposed to keep me safe from gruff arcaners with gorgeous shoulders and soft lips that promised the world. My belly dipped at the ghost of his lips on mine, at the memory of his body wrapped around me, his hands palming my ass, his rather impressive erection pressing against my center.

Come on, my beautiful little bird. What's my name?

Goose bumps tightened all over my body. His wild scent still filled the small room, and I had to get the hell out of there before I did something stupid. Like swoon or think I could be normal or plan for the future.

Shaking my head, I snatched the cleaning supplies and marched out of the closet. The dining hall wasn't the cleanest place in the world. The tables were always slightly sticky, the floor could use a good sweeping, and the chairs had this film on them that made me shudder every time I sat down.

Gross.

Though, I had the feeling that Acosta—*Nico*—didn't give a shit if I cleaned anything at all as long as I was far, far away from all the other instructors while magic was in play. The cold fear of breaking one of those potion bottles slapped me in the face as I sprayed cleanser on the closest table.

If Nico hadn't gotten me out of there—if he hadn't believed me...

I could have really hurt someone. This fucked-up magic could have caused some real destruction. Not just an apothecary. Not just a fire.

I could have killed someone.

My vision blurred as the reality of the situation set in. If Nico couldn't find something to help—something to tamp down whatever horrible magic squirmed beneath my skin—I couldn't stay here.

For the first time in my life, I actually had more than Ellie as a friend. I had Fiona and Hannah and Malia.

What if the wards fell and they did magic around me? What if I hurt one of them?

Blinking away tears, I furiously scrubbed the table.

What the hell was I going to do?

Reality eclipsed the small bit of happiness I'd had in that closet. If Nico didn't come back with something that would help before tomorrow—not that I thought he would find one in such a scant bit of time—I was leaving.

I couldn't go back to Savannah, of course, but there had to be somewhere in the world with no magic, no arcaners, no way I could hurt someone. Maybe not in Georgia, but there were places.

Right?

The small slice of hope I'd felt at Nico's promise crumbled to ash in my chest.

Because where the hell could I go with no money?

And no ride?

And no real place to go?

And the ABI looking to kill me the first chance they got?

Because that was what they did to arcaners who were a danger to every single person they came into contact with. That's what they did to the anomalies.

The freaks. The ones they couldn't pin down or shove in a box or control.

So I sprayed cleanser and I scrubbed and I tried to come up with a plan that kept me alive and everyone safe. By the time I was done, I had the first leg of a shaky strategy. It was weak at best, but it was better than nothing.

"If you scrub that table any harder, you're going to wear the paint right off it," Fiona said right by my ear, scaring the absolute shit out of me.

Shaking and weak-kneed, I slid into the closest upright chair and fought off the urge to spray cleanser at her like a misbehaving cat. "You suck, Fi. You really, really do."

"I'm not the one who was off in la-la land for who knows how long. You've been here for hours, chickadee. We done had lunch and everything while you've been over here working your little tail off. What gives?"

Oh, how to answer that question. "Acosta sentenced me to cleaning this pigsty, so that's what I've been doing."

Yes, I paired that with a shrug and a nonchalant tone, and I was not nervous or obvious about the fact that I was lying my ass off at all.

Totally.

Fiona jutted out a hip and planted her dainty hand

on it, her purple polished nails looking like she'd just come from a salon. I was lucky my shoes were on the right feet, and she had time to paint her nails?

"I know I'm blonde, but blind and stupid, I am not." She stepped forward, dropping her voice to a whisper. "The range? What happened?"

Finding my feet, I went back to my scrubbing, moving onto the next table. "I don't know what you mean."

"Don't you dare piss on my leg and tell me it's raining." She rested her hip against the table and snatched the dirty cloth right out of my hand. "One second, potion bottles are exploding and there's fire everywhere, and the next, you're over the null line with Instructor Smexy Pants and the fire is out."

"Instructor Smexy Pants?"

She pointed at her face. "Not. Blind. Have you *seen* those buns? They are juicy enough to take a bite out of. Alas, all he's been doing for the last four days is staring at *you*, so I figure I've already lost my shot." She flicked the rag at me. "And don't change the subject."

Wincing, I fought off the urge to spray her. At the beginning of this, she'd said she didn't want to talk about our families, but if I was going to explain, there was no other way around it. "Does the name Bannister mean anything to you?"

It was a stupid question. Ames had shouted my name for all the world to hear about a zillion times over the last four days. And by the way Fi's eyes widened, she'd already heard about my family, my crime, *and* my sentence. She schooled her features from out-and-out shock to something resembling nonchalance.

"No," she fibbed, "can't say as I have."

Snatching the rag back, I gave her a grateful glance and got back to scrubbing. "Liar."

Fiona sighed like I'd really caught her in the mother of all cover-ups. "Okay, fine. Everyone—*and I do mean everyone*—has heard about the Bannister who started the Azalea Apothecary fire. Though, word on the street is that it was an explosion that leveled half of Savannah, but you and I both know that's not true."

Leveled half of Savannah? Shit on a stick. I'm going to have to change my name now.

"It was *one* apothecary, *no one* died, and I *tried* to tell that dipshit not to cast around me, but..." Funny, I'd told that exact same story to the council that handed down my sentence, but they seemed rather reluctant to hear me out.

There were seven arcane councils in this country, one in Savannah, New Orleans, Knoxville, Sedona, Salem, Portland, and San Francisco. And I just so happened to get the one that was the least lenient, least tolerant of my oddities, and least willing to listen to a damn thing I had to say.

"Well, that's what happens when I'm around magic. One little smoke bomb turns into an inferno. One healing spell blows up an apothecary. You get the picture."

Fiona tapped on her lip with a shiny purple nail. "You know, I've never heard of anyone being born with magic that wonky. You think one of your parents pissed someone off and you got cursed or something? Because that would make a hell of a lot more sense. The Bannister name brings its fair share of hate."

Her theory had merit—however, I'd been this way all my life. Even before the usual puberty bitch-slap of arcane magic that most witches get, I was still causing a ruckus. If Fiona knew how many times I was told to go outside or to Ellie's so my family could have a "single moment of peace," well, she'd get that sad look on her face, and I just couldn't deal with that right now.

"I've always been this way. As long as I can remember." Blinking back frustrated tears, I moved to the next table.

Nico wasn't going to find a thing to help me. He couldn't. Because if he could, then what did that say about my family? With all their power and influence and clout that they'd rather me go on this way than get fixed?

That they'd let me suffer.

And for what?

No, Nico wasn't going to find anything because there wasn't anything to find. And because he wouldn't, I needed to leave. Just get gone before someone figured me out and killed me on the spot.

"But surely someone can help. Have you as—"

Whirling, I slapped the bottle of cleanser on the table. "Yes," I whispered. "I've asked my parents. And my grandmother. And my aunts. And anyone else I could possibly think of to help me. My family is either incapable or not interested in making me a functional member of their coven. And since they have cut off all contact and let my ass swing in the wind at my trial, I'm pretty sure they don't give a shit if I ever do. I can count on one hand the number of people in my life that care if I lived or died."

And as soon as I started causing problems, the number would whittle down to just Ellie and Alice. They were the only people who didn't make me feel like a monster or a leper or unwanted. And if I left, I'd be losing that, too.

But even if I didn't leave, how long could I use them

as a crutch? How long would it be until I couldn't even have that?

Fuck. It shouldn't be this hard, right? To live?

"Wren," Fiona cooed. "There are far more people that care about you than you think. And hey, maybe I can ask somebody? I know we Jacobs's aren't as hoity-toity as ya'll Bannisters, but there must be something someone can do, right?"

Shrugging, I gave her my best smile—the same one I gave Ellie when she said thank you for saving her mother. The same one when she apologized over and over for what happened. Ellie shouldn't have felt guilty for what happened in that fire any more than Fiona should feel pity about the family I couldn't change.

And just like with Ellie, I told Fiona the same damn thing. "Don't worry about it. It'll be fine. It always is."

Fiona, however, was harder to shake. "Again, woman. It ain't raining. Let's get you some food, huh? Classes are over anyway, and this place never looked so good. What do you say?"

Frowning, I finally took a look around. I was on the last table, and it was sparkling. So was every chair and the stainless-steel buffet. The windows were free of dust and grime, and the floor was spotless. An ache settled in between my shoulder blades and a gentle throb made itself known in my hands.

"Ya'll ate lunch here? Without me noticing?" I spotted a yellow rolling bucket filled with filthy water. When had I mopped?

"Hell, no. Malia and Hannah made everyone eat outside after they caught Patrick and Roman handing you cleaning supplies. Evidently, you were preoccupied with *something*, because as soon as one of those yahoos handed you a broom, you started attacking the floor. Same with the mop. Then when you ran out of floor to clean, you went back to scrubbing tables."

So that super-secret planning session I'd had where I'd mapped out my escape and everything, hadn't been as private as I'd thought.

Super.

Hopefully, I'd at least done it silently.

"You were in the zone," Fiona continued, ushering me away from the table I'd been attacking. "I've never seen anyone but my mama do that right before she blasted my daddy for some dumb shit he'd said."

She snatched the mop handle and guided the rolling bucket toward the janitor's closet. Gods, I had to be a mess if she was treating me with kid gloves. She dumped the water into the giant tub sink, and in the quiet of the room where I'd kissed Nico all those hours ago, the real interrogation began.

"So, what's going on with you and Acosta? Does he know about... *everything*?"

Oh, how to answer her.

"He knows enough." Hell, he knew more than I did if he could find a way to keep me from exploding the whole freaking camp. But what was going on with us?

Even I didn't know that.

Studying the shelf filled with cleaning products, I ignored her pointed stare.

"And?" Fiona's gaze was likely to burn a hole in my cheek.

"And nothing. He knows about my problem. He thinks he can fix it, but he can't. And when the other instructors find out that I'm a walking, talking time bomb, they'll kick me out so fast I'll likely leave chem trails upon my exit."

Or blood from my inevitable execution. That was a very real possibility, too. Why was I still here again?

She dropped the bucket back in the sink with a clatter, and attack-hugged me until I squeaked. "Then let's hope he's right. I just found my people, you know. Can't have ya'll hauling off and getting kicked out already."

My smile was brittle as I hugged her back. Because I couldn't get kicked out of here if I left, now, could I?

I think Fiona knew I was planning something,

because a few hours later, I'd finally convinced her I was fine enough to be left alone. This was after she'd stuffed me full of food, I'd managed to take a tepid shower, and I'd "rested."

Trust me, there was no rest to be had in this cabin—not with the contingency plans that circled on loop in my brain.

As soon as I was sure Fiona, Hannah, and Malia were out of earshot, I opened my wall locker and started packing my duffle. I didn't have much—just some clothes and toiletries, a few first aid items—so the bag was no fuller than when I'd started. Smartly, I left all the ABI trainee uniforms, boots, and insignia right where they lay.

I wasn't going to need them, now, was I?

As fast as I could, I got dressed in jeans, two pairs of thick socks, and my now-clean boots. Then I shoved my arms in a tank, a thin, long-sleeved shirt, and threw on a jacket. I was tempted to stuff one of the itchy wool blankets in my pack, but I knew if it got wet, it would only weigh me down.

I foresaw a ton of walking in my future, and my only hope was that my feet could actually take it this time. Then I waited, pretending to sleep until the entire camp was quiet and I could make my escape. It took a while, but once Hannah's snores started, I figured I was in the clear.

Sliding out of my bed, I gently pulled my duffle from underneath and minced to the back door and took a final look around. Fiona laid in a sprawled heap on her bed, a perfectly pedicured foot hanging off the mattress. She was a tiny hurricane, her area always haphazard and half-undone.

Hannah's snores ramped up, and I took that as my cue to scoot before she woke herself up. Slipping from the cabin, I shouldered my duffle and gently pushed the door closed, careful not to make a noise. There were plenty of arcaners that could hear my very heartbeat even under the null wards, so silence was the name of the game here.

Picking my way into the tree line, I managed to remain unseen, keeping to the shadows. The night was just on the warm side of chilly, and I thanked the stars above I managed to remember a jacket. I needed to get as much distance from the camp as I could before my bed got discovered empty, but first I needed to make it down the stupid mountain in one piece.

The gentle rumble of a pair of male voices stopped me in my tracks. Caught in the middle of a cleared trail, I whipped my head this way and that to try and find a big enough tree to hide behind. And the voices were getting closer. Without much grace, I shuffled behind a large oak, slowly taking my pack off before the bright-purple canvas gave me away.

"I don't get what's the big deal. She's fair game as far as I'm concerned."

Ames. And, without a doubt, that fucker was talking about me.

"You need to back off," Girard replied, his tone sharp as a razor. "It's bad enough I have instructors coming in my office bitching about you, but I have students doing it, too. Do you know how bad you have to fuck up that students are risking their entire careers to tattle on an instructor?"

Their steps faltered, stuttering to a stop very close to my tree. Covering my mouth so I didn't make a sound, I tried to keep my breaths from coming in the frightened pants of a girl damn near caught.

One wrong move, and I was screwed. One sound and they'd find me.

"I don't know how she got those girls to follow her, but you have to—"

"It was an entire cabin. Of *male* students," Girard hissed, cutting Ames off.

"Then she's fucking them," Ames insisted, his petulant, scolded little boy tone grating my ears. "She has to be. She snared them just like she did Acosta. You've seen him watching her. You *know* there's something going on."

Shame and rage and a fair bit of revulsion shot through me at once. I fought off the urge to jump from my hiding place and punch Ames right in his stupid, bitch-ass mouth. Okay, so fighting off the urge was taking far more effort than I'd have liked. Digging my fingernails into the tree bark, I held myself there, barely breathing, barely moving.

And worse?

There were a pair of golden eyes staring at me through the trees. I froze, staring at the shining eyes, trying not to give myself away to the men on the other side of the tree, and praying whatever the fuck it was that had eyes that bright in the middle of this pitch blackness didn't eat me.

"Oh, give it a rest," Girard barked, making me flinch. "That girl barely has time to wipe her own ass let alone fuck an entire cabin. You've made sure of that. Back. Off. Or I'm going to have to report you to your collective and your superior. What strike are you on, Ames?"

Warlocks—what few there were of them—belonged to collectives. Like a witch's coven, they were filled with family and leaders, rules and regulations. Not that I'd ever actually belonged to any coven whatsoever, but I got the gist. To get reported to one's collective carried the same weight as getting charged by the ABI, and the punishments were severe.

And all that was going on in the back of my mind as I watched those fucking eyes get closer.

"Bu—" Ames began, only to be cut off with something that sounded an awful lot like a gurgle.

"Back. Off. Don't make me say it again."

Ames must have nodded or something, because the conversation ended, and their footsteps resumed.

And all the while, those golden eyes got closer and closer until the thing attached to them stepped into the faint light of the full moon filtering through the leaves. Peaked ears covered in gray fur led to a longish muzzle and a regal face—all awesome until I realized the very large apex predator stalking casually toward me.

It was a wolf.

A giant, gray killing machine with glowing golden eyes. My heart tripped inside my chest. There were wolves in Savannah, sure, but I'd never seen one, and I sure as hell didn't know how to not get killed by one, either. Stumbling, I moved, ready to scream my head off when that wolf wasn't thirty feet away anymore.

It was right next to me, a gray mist coating its fur as its body changed shape.

Then I was flat on my back in the dirt with Nico on

top of me, his warm hand covering my mouth. And despite the fact that his body was on top of mine, and his arms were wrapped around me, the expression on his face was *not* happy.

No, I had a feeling I was in real deep shit.

Wren's fear wrenched at the hold I had on my wolf, the animal so close to the surface, so recently in the driver's seat, it nearly stole all my control. Her wide green-gold eyes peered up at me as her scent filled my nose, and I fought off the urge to yell.

She was supposed to stay put. She was supposed to wait for me. I swore to her I was coming back with a solution to our—*her*—problem and here she was in the woods, nearly caught, nearly hurt, nearly...

"Going somewhere?" I growled through my teeth, forcing my hand off her mouth now that Ames and Girard were out of earshot. Wren's skin remained white for a moment until it flushed pink, the pressure of my hand on her too much, and that earned me a solid dose of shame until the guilt on her face finally registered.

The men's steps faded into the distance too far for them to hear anything we had to say. And if Wren was smart, she should start talking anytime now...

She sucked in a shuddering breath, likely unable to take a full one with my body on top of hers, but I was having a hard enough time not shifting as it was. Pinning her down was the last hold I had on my sanity at the moment.

"Yes," she breathed, her bottom lip trembling as tears pooled in her eyes. "I... I was leaving."

Just her admitting it had my gut falling to the ground and my chest caving in. Heat flashed over my skin as I gritted my teeth against the burn.

"Why?" I ground out, my jaw locked so I didn't toss my head back and howl. My wolf was too close, too in control, too powerful. With the moon full and my thirtieth birthday minutes away, not shifting seemed to be more and more impossible by the second.

Wren shook her head, shoving at my shoulders, and I fought off the urge to press into her more, to pin her down, to mark her with my teeth.

So no matter where she went or who she ran into, they would all know she was mine.

Mine.

But that was the wolf talking, not me.

Rolling off her, I found my feet, careful not to step into the moonlight. The last thing I needed was for that fucking moon to hit me again. Hell, I couldn't even look at her—couldn't stand the reminder that she was trying to run. And if I saw that gods-forsaken purple duffle again...

She was going to leave me.

"Because I didn't trust that you'd find anything to help," she finally answered, a kick in the gut if there ever was one. But then she continued, and the hits just kept on coming. "Because I don't want to hurt anyone. Because I don't want to die. You told me so yourself. They're going to kill me, Nico. And they will as soon as they find out what's wrong with me."

I swallowed thickly, the truth in her words as sharp as a razor, and I tilted my head back to stare at the forest canopy. The moon threatened to trickle through the leaves, and no matter how much we wolves said we weren't moon-called, the truth would come out eventually. Even then the moon beckoned me, begged me to let my wolf free, pleaded to let its silver beams fall on my skin.

Fisting my fingers, I shoved everything down—all the fear, the rage, the pain. "And what if I did find something? What if I commissioned someone to help?

What if I risked everything to make sure you were safe, huh?"

Bitterness threatened to sink me. I'd done exactly what I'd said I'd do, and where was she? Not where she said she'd be—where I told her to be. I'd nearly woken up every girl in that cabin when I'd realized she was gone, only to find her in the fucking woods, not three paces away from Ames.

He could have caught her.

He could have killed her.

He could have...

Didn't she understand the danger?

Her gasp had me spinning to face her, lunging to catch her as she wilted to the earth. Her fingers found the threads of my shirt, yanking at it like she was trying to burrow into my skin. The weight of the amulet in my pocket seemed like such a trivial thing to me.

It was inconsequential. Insignificant. But to Wren, it was everything.

"Yo-you did? You found something?" Pain ravaged her features, tempered only by the faint traces of relief. Tears spilled down her face, as the scent of agony burned my nose. With a shaking hand, she pressed it against the skin of my cheek. "Thank you. Thank you."

Her whole body trembled, and I couldn't have stopped myself from kissing her even if I tried.

My lips found hers, taking her mouth, her scent. It filled my nose, that jasmine and honeysuckle perfume that was all Wren as I tasted the sweetness on her tongue. My fingers found her braid, curling the red rope of her hair around my fist as I devoured her mouth, swallowing her moans like a man starved. She nipped at my bottom lip, the bite of the sting calling forth fangs of my own.

I wanted to sink them into her neck, marking her for all the world to see.

She's mine.

My wolf howled inside my head making me break the kiss, my breath mingling with hers. Unable to stop myself, I lifted my gaze to the canopy of trees, a single beam of moonlight falling to the forest floor. Finding my feet, I clasped her hand in mine as it called to me, beckoning me closer.

It was time—one I couldn't fight or say no to.

Normally, wolves were home on this night, knowing that once the moon hit us on our thirtieth birthday, our lives would change forever. If we were lucky, we knew our mate. If we were really lucky, we at least liked them. But there was always a chance that they'd died, or they were married to someone else, or they didn't want you back.

"Nico? What's happening?"

But I couldn't tell her. My wolf was driving this train and Wren and I were simply passengers. Pulling her behind me I strode toward that beam of light as if it were a siren call. Funny, because the woman behind me was the same, her song her scent, and exactly like those poor sailors, I would be crashing soon enough.

As soon as the light hit me, I knew I'd fucked up. I dropped Wren's hand as I fell to my knees, the searing heat of the light on my skin like the worst of burns. My wolf writhed under my flesh, aching to be set free, but I managed to keep him in check. What I could not do was stop his fangs from filling my mouth and his talons from erupting from my fingertips.

Shifting never felt like this. There was no pain, no agony. No bones breaking and reforming. But now? Now everything hurt, everything was on fire.

"Nico?" Wren called, her cool hands on my face as I tried not to howl.

Curling my arms around her legs, I clutched her to me as I tried to ride out the worst of it. But I didn't even know what this was. I had a vague idea of this being the mating and the rest of my alpha power coming to me, but no one had ever said it would be like this.

No one said it would hurt this bad.

No one said I would want to scrape my own skin off at the same time I wanted to bathe in her scent. And I did. I wanted the gentle perfume of Wren's skin all over me. I wanted her taste on my tongue, her moans in my mouth, her hair in my fist.

Burying my face in her belly, I soaked in her scent as I rode out the worst pain I'd ever felt. Another lash hit me, and I tightened my hold, earning me a gasp. She bent, curling herself around me as she held on, murmuring soft words and gentle shushes as she ran her fingers through my hair.

Somehow, she got on my level, her knees bumping against mine as I pulled her closer.

Mine. Mate. Mine. Mate. Mine, mine, mine.

That scent filled my nose, the one that was only Wren's—only hers and no one else's. Only she would do. Only she could quell this ache in my chest, this burn in my skin. Only she could soothe the beast in me.

I wanted to tell her what was happening—I did—but the words wouldn't come. The only thing I managed to get out was, "*Mine.*"

Those green-gold eyes widened, her perfect lips forming a small "O" of surprise, and I wanted to bite that plump bottom lip. Banding my arm around her back, I curled my other hand under her braid at the base of her skull. Wren's eyelids drooped as her scent sweetened, her gaze falling to my mouth before she closed the distance between us.

And now I understood why it hurt so bad.

I'd been holding myself back, making sure it was her choice—*I* was her choice. As soon as her lips brushed mine, the burn began to ease. Starving for her, the kiss went from a gentle brush to the pair of us doing our level best to devour each other. Wren wrapped her arms around my neck as my hands found their way to the back of her thighs. Yanking them up, she snaked those legs around my waist, and it was better than I dreamed it would be.

In less than a second, I found my feet, taking her with me, not once breaking the kiss. I pressed her back against the closest tree, missing the moonlight already. The heat of her sex filtered through our clothes and into my cock and I couldn't help my groan. She swallowed it with a gasp, her hips bucking at the contact.

Pressing into her further, I let my fingers explore, sneaking under the hem of her thin shirt to touch her soft skin. Even against the rough pads of my fingers, the curve of her waist was like the warmest silk. Her breath stuttered as I cupped her ribs and nearly stopped altogether when I flicked my thumb over her tight nipple.

Wren broke the kiss, gasping for breath and I took that opportunity to taste her neck, trailing nibbling kisses down the column of her throat. Her scent sweetened further, turned heady with her desire—her want

—for me. Her pulse fluttered against my lips as her nails scraped my scalp, her hold tightening on my hair.

Mine.

I needed inside her, needed to sink into her softness, her heat. My wolf and I both craved it, near mindless from it. And as Wren writhed in my grip, her hips circling, pressing herself against the straining cock in my jeans, my control was slipping.

And fast.

Fumbling, I yanked at her jacket and somehow, we managed to get it off her arms, discarding it somewhere far away from her skin. Wren wiggled, pushing at my hold and somehow my brain got the message, and I relinquished my hold on her.

No. She's saying no.

My chest wanted to cave in on itself, but as soon as her feet found the forest floor, she tore off her shirt, revealing acres of pale skin for me to worship. In an instant, her bra was gone, the light-blue confection only in my way. My mouth found the peak of her nipple, the cinnamon bud just as sweet as the rest of her.

We fumbled together, unzipping jeans, shoving clothing aside, and before I knew it, I'd spun her in my arms, the curve of her luscious ass against my aching cock. One hand was full of her ample breast and the other cupped her jaw, tilting her head just so I could bury my nose in the crook of her neck. My fangs ached, ready to take her as mine before something told me to stop.

Ask. Don't just take. Ask her.

Through the mindlessness, through the lust and pheromones and just plain magic, I managed to grab hold of my sanity.

I tilted her head, making her look at me, watching her glorious green-gold eyes flare as they met mine. "Tell me you want this," I ordered, my voice rough with the ghost of my wolf. "Tell me you're mine. Tell me you want me."

As soon as she said yes—*if* she said yes—my mark would be on her forever.

She would be mine forever.

And I would be hers.

Nico's eyes glowed with his wolf as he waited for my response, his whole body practically vibrating with need. I didn't know why he was so upset I'd tried to leave or what had made him feel so much pain in the moonlight.

Tell me you want this. Tell me you're mine. Tell me you want me.

His words seemed to mean something, resonating with a power I didn't understand. But I couldn't think with his lips so close—couldn't focus on anything but the heat of his skin against mine and his hand on my breast and the delicious way he made me look at him, forcing my chin up so there was no other option but to stare into those gorgeous golden eyes.

Maybe it was the way he said it, the desire to be

wanted in return that sealed it for me, but my acceptance fell from my lips before my brain even had time to think of the consequences.

"Yes," I breathed against his mouth, and his hold tightened. "I want you. I want this. *Please*."

His hand left my breast as he positioned his cock at my slick opening. He could breathe in my direction, and I'd be ready for him. His kisses, his hands on me? I was done for.

He hovered on the edge, the teasing pressure earning a whimper from me as he hesitated. I wanted him inside me, his groans in my ears, and his kiss on my tongue.

"Tell me you're mine," he growled, nipping at my bottom lip with his sharp teeth. "No one else gets you this way. No one else, Wren."

I knew next to nothing about Nico—other than his last name and the fact that he was a wolf, an ABI agent, and he had a keen interest in keeping me alive. But right then, I didn't care about what I didn't know or what my words might mean. I didn't care about anything other than letting him do whatever he wanted with me.

"Yes," I hissed, trying and failing to rock my hips back to take him in. His hard grip stopped me, and even that made me moan.

"Say it, my beautiful little bird. Tell me you're mine."

It felt like I was agreeing to something far more binding than I could comprehend, but I needed him inside me. I needed him to fill me up, to hold me, to bite me, to...

"I'm yours," I murmured, loving the way my lips brushed his as I spoke.

"That's my good girl." Nico wasted no time—as soon as those words passed my lips, he plunged inside, filling me full, with one long stroke. He swallowed my gasp as he pressed a searing kiss to my mouth, his tongue dancing with mine.

He pulled out, and I whimpered at the loss until he slammed back in, the force of it rocking me up on my toes. We fell forward against the thick oak tree, his forearm protecting my delicate skin from the roughness of the bark.

His hand left my hip, trailing down in between my legs to my sex. He played me like a well-tuned instrument, pressing on my clit with the perfect pressure. Pleasure seared through me as his strokes picked up speed. I was stretched to bursting with his searing hot moans in my ear, his beautiful fingers playing in the slick wetness at my center.

My legs began to tremble, my orgasm racing for me —too big, too much, too...

"Nico," I gasped, a warning, a plea. I needed more—more of him. "Please."

"You gonna come for me?" he growled in my ear, his voice deepening ever so slightly as it vibrated through my chest.

The best I could do was nod, but even that was feeble. I curled my arms behind me, clutching whatever I could reach, trying to hold on.

"Show me how pretty you come, beautiful. Show me."

As if on command, my release hit, slamming into me with enough force to weaken my legs, to make me scream. Fire raced over every inch of my skin, lighting up every nerve ending, every cell. Then Nico struck, his fangs burying into the delicate skin of my shoulder. It should have hurt, the skin breaking under the razor-sharp points of his teeth, but all I felt was a wave of bliss as he roared out his release.

His thrusts gentled and he found my lips, the taste of my blood coppery on his mouth. I nipped at his bottom lip—hard—my teeth breaking the skin. Nico's blood mingled with mine, our kiss never once stopping, even as he pulled himself from me. Spinning in his arms, he pressed me against the tree, the rough bark against my skin making me moan.

Everything felt good—every cell in my body dialed toward pleasure. I'd just had the mother of all releases, and yet, I was starving for him, needing him again, even though I'd just had him. The heat of his bare chest against mine nearly killed me. It was as if I'd been drugged.

Nico broke the kiss, cupping my jaw in his hands as he stared down into my eyes. "I hope you were topped up on sleep. Because I don't think either of us are getting any tonight."

My sex clenched, aching for him again. "Promise?"

Leisurely, we righted our clothing, dropping kisses to all the skin in reach. After we'd found my jacket and bra, Nico shouldered my duffle, pulling me by the hand behind him as we headed back to camp. Only at the thought of going back, did the euphoria lift.

"I can't go back," I whispered, my feet stuttering to a stop. Nico had said he *might* have found something to help. I'd taken him at his word, but that was then, and this was now.

A scowl marred his perfect brow, and he let go of my hand to reach into his pocket. He pulled out a black velvet drawstring bag. "I went to Savannah. Talked to Carmichael. He admitted that you didn't start the fire." He pulled the bag open and dumped something into his palm. "In exchange for my silence, I had him make you this."

Nico pulled at the metal, drawing up the chain of a necklace, the yellow stone winking at me in the dark. "Your own personal null ward. It won't grant you any powers, but it will keep you from affecting everyone else's. It was the best I could do under the circumstances."

Shakily, I reached for the necklace. Something so simple, so easy. A null ward. Why hadn't I thought of that?

Tears filled my eyes as my fingers closed around the metal. All this time, every worry, every misstep, and it all could have been solved by a fucking necklace? Under the null wards already, I didn't feel any different when I held the metal, didn't feel any magic coming from the jewelry at all.

"How do we know it works on me?" All the bliss I'd felt moments ago was gone, now replaced with a lifetime of fear. Because things not working around me wasn't exactly new.

"Carmichael tested it himself, but we'll know for sure tomorrow. You'll have to retake the potion bomb iteration with Ames. And hey, if it doesn't work, I'll get you out of here, get you safe. Promise."

Nico plucked the chain from my hand and clasped it

around my neck. "I won't let them hurt you, Wren. And I won't let you hurt anyone else."

The cool metal rested between my breasts, a gentle reminder that he'd gone all the way to Savannah and back for me. He'd hunted down Carmichael. He'd...

No one—not ever—had done something like that for me. Pursing my lips, I looked him over. "What—exactly—is your stance on blow jobs? Are they just okay, or are they like Christmas?"

Because if anyone in the history of ever deserved to be taken care of, it was Nico.

He banded an arm around my back, dipping his head to my ear. "I have a feeling anything you want to do to me will rock my fucking world, but if you want to suck my cock to show your gratitude, I won't stop you. I think you'll look fucking beautiful on your knees for me."

Forty minutes, a perilous trek through the camp, and a shower later, I found myself naked on my knees in Nico's bed. His back was propped against the headboard, his legs spread wide with me in between them. He'd already given me another mind-melting orgasm in the shower with his fingers, and I was eager to make him beg for me.

His fist was wrapped in my hair, not pushing, not guiding, simply there, letting me tease him with my mouth. I laved the underside of his cock with my tongue, running it over the sensitive spot just under the head. A growl erupted from his chest—not the fake kind men used when they were riled up but a real wolf one—animalistic and sexy as hell.

"Stop teasing me, beautiful," Nico snarled, and I figured fucking with him would earn me a glorious punishment.

Swirling my tongue around the tip, I bobbed my head, sucking him deep before popping off. "I don't know, teasing you is mighty fun."

I went back to work, taking him deep until he was a writhing mess ready to come at any second. Then like the absolute asshole I was, I drew off him, running my tongue up the underside in the softest of teases.

"What did you say in the woods? Oh, that's right," I murmured, giving his cock a quick suck. "Tell me you're mine. That this is mine and no one else's."

Up until that moment, I hadn't quite comprehended just how fast Nico could move. Before I knew it, I was flat on my back in his bed with a very serious wolf in my face. Without an ounce of artifice, he answered me, "I thought this was implied, but I'll confirm it for you. I'm yours. My cock is yours—my body is yours and no one else's."

His rough palm ran over the skin of my thigh right

before he spread me wide, fitting himself in between my legs. Slowly, he dipped his fingers into my folds, gently pressing against my clit. "Such a pretty pussy. I should taste it."

He worked his thick fingers inside me, hooking, pressing against the bundle of nerves just right to make me writhe. A moment later, he filled my mouth with those same fingers, making me taste myself as I sucked them clean. Then his mouth was on mine, his tongue sweeping inside to savor me. I only had his lips for a moment before he trailed them down my body, worshiping every inch of skin he came across, and then he was between my legs again.

Instantly, I regretted teasing him. If I was good at the game, Nico was a master. Before he was done, I was a babbling mess, pleading for him to just fuck me already.

And he did. Nico fucked me, made love to me, defiled me, and ravaged me in every position I could possibly think of and about twelve I had no idea existed. He wrapped me around his little finger, making me forget any lover before him and assuring there wouldn't be another after him.

As the sun threatened to crest the horizon, I'd confirmed two things. One: I was stupidly infatuated with a wolf shifter. Like falling all over myself, I didn't know how I was going to function around him, puppy-dog eyed and completely stupid, infatuated. Two: Keeping this under my hat was going to be the death of me.

But unlike in so many occasions before, I was pretty sure I was fucked in the good way this time.

CHAPTER 13

NICO

If it weren't for the sun threatening to crest the horizon, I could have stayed in this bed for the foreseeable future. For the first time since Wren blazed into my life, my wolf was quiet. The scent of her all over me—in my nose, on my skin—soothed him in a way I'd never felt before. It was oddly peaceful to have him so docile, so calm.

It also scared the absolute shit out of me.

A week ago, I'd been lamenting that there was no way Wren could have been my mate—no way the universe could be that cruel. Now, I knew there was nothing I wouldn't do to protect her—nothing that I wouldn't sacrifice, no one I wouldn't kill. Hadn't I proved that already? Too bad protecting her right then came in the form of waking her up and getting her back to her cabin, preferably without my scent all over her.

My wolf roused at that thought, and I couldn't blame him. Wren washing off my scent made my gut hurt, but that was the problem with this mixed bag of arcaners. Too many could smell me on her and confuse what it meant—think badly of her and I both, not realizing who she was to me.

If we were in a den, it would be different. If we were with my family, we'd be congratulated, the mate bond so powerful to my kind that it was deeper than any other vow we could have taken.

But Wren was a witch—an ousted one at that. And that made her a target here.

Dipping my head, I breathed her in, pressing my nose into her hair as she continued to use me as a body pillow. The copper strands were a tangled mess, scenting of her sweat, orgasms, and the traces of her desire. My arms tightened around her as if even they had no intention of letting her go. My mouth, however, had other plans.

"It's time to wake up, beautiful."

She snuffled, hiding her face against my chest as she moaned her dissent. I couldn't blame her. Other than a few cat naps here and there, neither of us had gotten anything close to a restful night.

"Okay," I conceded, settling in. "You can sleep in, but that's only if you don't mind every person within a mile radius knowing just how many times you came last night."

That did the trick. Wren shoved against my chest, spearing me with one bleary eye. "What?"

Tapping my nose, I murmured, "We smell of sex, my beautiful bird. And anyone else with a decent sense of smell will know exactly what we did last night, too."

Both of her eyes widened as she sat up, pulling the sheet with her to cover her breasts. "I have a feeling sleeping with my instructor is not the best way to stay in this program, correct?"

My teasing smile fell. While that thought was always at the back of my mind, I didn't want Wren agonizing over her safety.

That was my job.

"No one is going to hurt you, Wren. I'll make sure of it," I murmured, cupping her cheek with my palm. "No one. But to stay on the safe side, let's shower and get you back to your cabin before anyone starts asking questions, yeah?"

Wren pressed her cheek against my hand, almost nuzzling it the way a wolf would, her body desperate for the contact that only a mate could give.

"You know, no one but Ellie and Alice have ever

promised me anything... my family... they didn't..." She shook her head, her lips pressing together so hard they turned white at the edges. Sniffing, she shoved herself from the bed and marched to the bathroom, not looking at me again.

Clenching my teeth, I fought off the urge to howl.

Wren's.

Fucking.

Family.

Margot Bannister was a piece of work, and Wren's grandmother was a thousand times worse. And her aunts? There was a reason the Bannister name wasn't exactly liked in and around Savannah, even if it was feared. If Wren was the black sheep—and I had no doubt she was with a curse like hers—she'd have been demeaned and degraded, chastised and discarded more times than she could likely even remember.

Without the first clue of what to say, I followed her into the bathroom. She'd already flipped on the tap and was testing the water for temperature, not looking up once as I entered the room. She knew I was there—her skin pebbling as soon as I stepped across the threshold —but she didn't say a word.

Maybe now wasn't the right time to talk about this, but she needed to know she wasn't alone anymore. "I know this is rich coming from someone like me, with a pack like mine, but fuck your family, Wren." She straightened, a skeptical expression marring her gorgeous face. "Fuck every last one of them. It's okay to cut them out like a cancer. It's okay to ignore them like they ignored you. It's okay to let them go."

She lifted her shoulder in an indelicate shrug and stepped into the shower, letting the warm water darken her copper strands to auburn. She raised her face to the spray, cutting off any words that she could have replied with. With nothing else for it, I followed her in, wrapping an arm around her middle and kissing her wet hair.

She settled back into me, resting her head on my shoulder.

"You ever ached for the approval of someone you hated?" Wren asked, not turning, not moving, just resting against me like I was the lone person in the world holding her up.

I thought about the relationship I had with my father—the fights, the challenges—but I didn't hate the man. "Not really. My dad and I butt heads sometimes, but I still love him. I couldn't imagine not having a whole pack at my back and in my business." I dipped my head and pressed a kiss to her temple. "But I get it— the need to feel wanted. To require basic respect."

"To you, it's a stranger. Someone who shouldn't

have a biological urge to give a shit. For me? It's my mom. You give a shit when you don't have to, and you did even *before* I blew you."

I'd never wanted to hug someone, while also dying to kiss them, while also doing my level best to not bust out laughing, while also needing to fuck every last bad thought out of their head before. "So, the bar is on the floor, then?"

Wren snorted, turning so her face was away from the spray. "The bar is on Satan's doorstep and even he thinks it's too fucking low."

Filtering my fingers through her hair, I cupped her head against my chest. "At least good old Satan and I agree about something."

We didn't have enough time for me to fuck all the bad thoughts away, but I still kissed her until she was smiling from ear to ear. By the time we got clean and dressed, the sun was really threatening to come up, and we had to race in the shadows to get her back to her cabin before anyone woke up.

It took everything in me not to kiss her again, to not mark my scent all over her. My wolf was not happy about it one bit but keeping her safe was far more important than my comfort. I'd just have to deal, and so would my wolf.

Mate.

Yeah, yeah, buddy. But keeping her safe is more important.

I so rarely talked to my wolf, but it sure as fuck was necessary now. Visions of dragging Wren back to my cabin and ripping the throats out of anyone who dared disturb us flashed in my brain.

Down, boy.

Before I forced myself to leave her, Wren grabbed my hand.

"Thank you," she murmured, her voice almost inaudible even to my ears. "For helping me, for last night, for... everything."

I couldn't help it—just like I couldn't stop myself from kissing her that first time or the moon calling her to be my mate—I pulled her in and met her surprised lips with mine, tasting her one last time before letting her go. Backing away, I watched her shoulder her duffle and slip inside her cabin, fighting my damn wolf the whole time.

An hour and a half later, I was in the dining hall trying very hard not to notice just how fucking clean everything was. Sure, I'd told Wren to make it look good for her "punishment," but I hadn't expected her to take a toothbrush to the fucking grout for fuck's sake. It explained the aches in her body that I'd leached away while she'd slept.

Plus, the whole place was filled with her scent now, and it was driving my wolf crazy. Okay, so it was driving me absolutely batshit, too, but it was easier to blame the wild animal under my skin than deal with the fact that I was absolutely enamored by a woman I'd just met.

No wonder bonded men were so fucking protective over their mates. I hadn't understood until last night—hadn't even begun to comprehend just how far I'd go for her. I'd thought the swamp incident was bad. I was a damn fool.

"Excuse me?" a soft voice called, snapping me out of my Wren-induced craze. "Instructor Acosta?"

Turning, I found a short cadet with a severe expression, her dark hair pulled into an impossibly tight bun and her hands covered in gloves. Cadet Malia Nadir was in Wren's cabin, and the gloves were necessary so she herself didn't go absolutely insane in a group environment. A psychometry witch, Nadir was valuable to the ABI for so many reasons, but I cared more that she looked about ready to bolt.

"What's up, cadet?" If it weren't for the deep stench of abject fear coating the air around her, I probably would have told her to leave me alone, but something told me not to.

Her gaze shifted around before she moved closer. "I

—*we*—have a huge problem. A girl is missing from my cabin. The other two girls went to go look for her, but I'm worried."

It was as if the bottom dropped out of my gut.

"Her bed is messed up as if she slept in it last night, and all her stuff is there—"

I didn't let the girl finish before I was off, racing for Wren's cabin as fast as my human legs would take me. I couldn't shift—not right then—but if what that girl said was true, I didn't know if I'd be able to hold onto this shape.

She left, anyway. I told her I would protect her, and she left. Sheleftsheleftsheleft.

My wolf was howling, and I gritted my teeth so I didn't follow suit, the burn in my stomach and ache in my chest almost too much to bear. Last night was too good to be true. Of course it was. No one found their mate before the turning. No one got them so soon. And she'd accepted me far too easily. I was a fucking idiot to think everything would work out.

Wren didn't want me—not really.

By the time I made it to her cabin, my wolf had wrenched control from me, falling into a scenting trance. Wren's was all over the place, but it was fresh, as if she'd just been here.

"Whoa, man. Are you okay?" Nadir asked, out of breath. "Your eyes are glowing, you know."

Unbidden, a growl rumbled from my throat. "Did she say anything to you before she left? Any clue as to where she went?"

I'd find her. I would... I'd find her and... And what? Beg her to want me? Beg her to stay?

The cadet shook her head, her dark bun not budging an inch. "No. We went to bed and then she just wasn't here this morning. We checked the showers and the dining hall —hell, even the range." She marched past me, pointing to a bed that wasn't Wren's. "And it *looks* like she slept here..."

The confusion melted away as soon as the screen door slapped against the frame and Wren's scent mixed with the slightly dead one of a ghoul. I spun on a heel, staring down a distraught Wren who was huffing like she'd run a marathon.

"We ran the perimeter," Dumond announced. "I didn't smell her once."

Wren approached like I was a wild animal ready to strike. Fuck, I probably was one. Because all I could do was stare at her like I'd done the night before while she was pressed against that fucking tree, so close to being caught. My emotions were a mess—I was a mess—and I was probably scaring the shit out of these cadets.

"Ni—*Acosta*? Are you okay?" My last name on Wren's lips did nothing to calm me. In fact, it made it so much worse. I was Nico to her.

Blinking hard, I shook myself. I could *not* grab her and hide her away from everyone. I could *not* kiss the shit out of her. I could *not* let anyone know we were together.

Keep Wren safe, you fucking idiot. It's your one goddamn job.

"Fine," I ground out, amazed I could do that much. "Tell me what happened."

The screen door slapped again, with Ames strolling in like he had any right to be here. "Yeah, Bannister. Why don't you tell us all what happened?"

Don't kill him. Don't do it.

By some grace of the gods, Wren didn't even look at him, ignoring the antagonistic fuck-stick like he wasn't even there. "I don't know," she breathed, shaking her head. "We woke up, and she wasn't here. I figured she went to shower or something. We all got dressed for the day, but Fi still hadn't come back." She chewed on her bottom lip and began blinking like she was trying to stave off tears. "We checked the dining hall and the laundry and then we went to see if she was in the latrine. That's when we started getting worried. Malia came to find you, and Hannah and I ran the perimeter. It's like she's just gone."

Nodding, I tried not to wince. Hannah and Wren's scent could possibly mask Jacobs', making it that much harder to find her. First the female instructors leaving, and now this? Wyatt was right: there had to be something going on here.

"Bullshit." Ames scoffed. "What? She wanted to fuck her boyfriend in one of the other cabins and had you three make a big stink ab—"

Heat tingled down my spine as the urge to snap became almost too big to ignore. "Shut. The fuck. Up." It took everything in my power to keep my claws off that fucker. I heard every word he'd said about Wren last night, and him echoing those thoughts right now? Well, I was all out of patience. "Cadets? I need you to get to your next iteration. I'll look into this. We'll find her."

Wren was absolutely ashen, along with Nadir and Dumond, staring at Ames like he was the damn devil. Well, Dumond seemed ready for an Ames-sized snack and Nadir seemed like she'd been hit by a truck, but the sentiment was still valid.

The cadets filed out with Wren taking the rear, her stricken face the last thing I saw before the door slapped once more against the frame. They left just in time for me to wrap a clawed hand around Ames' throat.

"What the fuck is wrong with you? A female cadet is missing, and you immediately think *slut*? Get your head out of your dick for about a millisecond, will ya?"

Squeezing his neck a little harder, I relished his face going purple before I let him go. Snapping it would have been so easy but killing him would be far too much paperwork. And no wonder he was on probation from his collective. With an attitude like that, it was a miracle they let him live.

"What's going on here?" Girard thundered from the doorway, likely wondering why Ames was gasping for air, and I was three steps past murderous.

Since Ames was incommunicado at the moment, I answered, "We have a missing student. The cadets all went to bed at the same time last night, but when they woke up this morning, one was missing. Her name is Fiona Jacobs, sir."

The Jacobs witch line was a big deal in the South, almost as big as the Bannister one. Not all of them had a squeaky-clean reputation, either.

Girard's jaw ticked. "And why is Ames on the ground?"

"In front of Jacobs' bunkmates, he suggested she was fraternizing with another student and not missing." I cleared my throat. "Only it was more colorful than that."

The older man's eye twitched. "I see." He looked down his nose at the warlock at our feet. "I believe we've had a discussion about your conduct, Ames. Is this something I'm going to need to report to your collective, or are you going to remove your head from your ass sometime this decade?"

Ames continued to gasp on the floor and Girard spared him another disgusted glance before returning his gaze to me. "I appreciate your quick action, Acosta, but Fiona Jacobs isn't missing. She left the program last night, electing to return to her family rather than continuing with us."

Interesting. A cadet—who was performing at the top end of her class—left without a word in the middle of the night, without her things. Not an explanation, not a goodbye. Nothing.

I smelled bullshit.

And that bullshit was coming right from the top.

Worry churned in my gut as I shifted from foot to foot, staring at the target. Standing at the range podium, I clung to the wood, instead of doing what I really wanted to do, which was punch Ames right in the throat.

She wanted to fuck her boyfriend in one of the other cabins...

Fiona was missing. *Missing.* And he just wanted to brush it off?

Add that to the fact I hadn't exactly gotten to field-test the amulet at my neck, and well... I was a little out of sorts.

And it wasn't like I had any backup. It was only me and Ames out here, and it went without saying that the guy gave me the creeps.

Outside of the null line, I felt naked, and without my class or any other supervision other than this bumbling asshat? Not. Good.

"I can't believe you get to retake this test, Bannister," he grumbled, opening the armory cabinet that held all the potion bombs. "If it were up to me, I would have failed you. Though, it just goes to show that you and your family get all the special treatment, don't you?"

I'd sort of figured Ames hated me because of my name. Being a staunch misogynist and an all-around prick, it made sense that he'd hate me for something I couldn't control.

Roughly, he yanked out a flat of glowing orbs, smacking them onto the podium like he was trying to break them.

Shakily, I grabbed a bright-blue one, praying I didn't blow my hand off or explode the entire place as my fingers closed around the glass. Though, since it was just me and Ames, if the necklace was a dud, it was the perfect time for it to malfunction.

"Any fucking day now, Bannister. I do have other shit to do." Then he chuckled, a dark, creepy laugh that sent chills racing down my spine. "But you do, too, don't you? You're so busy fucking your classmates that I bet you've got plenty on your plate."

My fingers tightened around the glass. He'd made

those same claims last night to Girard, sullying my name just because he was butt-hurt about whatever the fuck was stuck up his ass.

"You going to try and fuck me for a good grade, too?" He moved closer, in my space, and dropped his voice to a whisper. "Does Acosta know you're throwing your cat at everyone? I bet the big, dumb wolf can't even smell them on you. So much for him being an alpha, huh? But you can't fool me. And as soon as I have proof, I'm getting you kicked out of here."

But kicking me out of this school didn't mean jail anymore.

It was a death sentence.

That fucker.

"Is that your go-to?" I said, a sneer firmly on my face as I backed up a step. "If a woman you don't like is doing better than *you* think she should, she's fucking everyone?"

Why that slipped out of my mouth, I didn't know, but I couldn't take one more stupid word. Right then, it didn't matter that he could get me kicked out. It didn't matter that he could use his power—both actual and perceived—against me. All that mattered was getting the absolute dumpster fire of a person to shut the fuck up.

Emboldened by the sheer rage churning in my gut—

which seemed to overtake the fear at the moment—I tossed the potion bomb in the air, catching it and tossing it again.

"You and I *both* know I don't get jail if this doesn't work out. I know what my paperwork says." I tossed the bottle again, my rage reaching the boiling point. "So, every time you say you're going to kick me out, you're threatening my life. And if I'm fucking literally *everyone* like you say? Then what's to stop me from going to my classmates—to Acosta—and having them all make sure you don't wake up tomorrow?"

Was that a step too far? Maybe, but I was done with Ames' shit. He threatened my life? Well, I was threatening his. And I was loving the wide-eyed sputtering and abject fear on his face.

"I'm a big, *bad* Bannister, right? I've got ties and connections, without an ounce of a conscience or a lick of scruples, and my life is on the line. I'm capable of just about anything, aren't I?"

The temptation to rip off the necklace Nico had given me and throw this fucking bomb at his feet—to watch him burn—would have scared the shit out of me if I were thinking clearly. But my mind was full of not finding Fiona, of racing around to try and find her. Of having Girard lie to my face and say she left of her own accord...

"I want you to think about that real hard before you open your mouth next time. Think about how good I am with a gun. Think about the potions exploding yesterday. Think about the apothecary that got me here." My smile was feral. "Soak it *all* in."

I tossed the potion again, practically giddy at Ames' gray face as he tracked the orb exactly like I had yesterday, praying it didn't explode.

It didn't matter that nearly everything I'd just said was complete bullshit—that fear, that worry, was priceless. It was about time he got back some of what he'd dished out.

"Or maybe you should do your fucking job and train me like you're supposed to without the sexual harassment and threats." Facing the target, I hauled my arm back and let the potion fly—not caring too much whether it actually exploded or not. "Just a thought."

The glass shattered on impact with the target, a gentle waft of smoke curled in the air before dissipating in the breeze just like it was supposed to. But I still saw Ames flinch out of the corner of my eye, and that was fabulous.

I wanted to feel the joy of the amulet working. Wanted to embrace the freedom it could bring me. But I couldn't focus on anything other than making Ames pay and Fiona.

Fiona.

What sucked? I now knew exactly how she would have felt seeing my bed empty and me nowhere to be found. I knew exactly what it was like to worry, and to wonder, and to not have a single shred of explanation.

Ames snatched the tray of potion bottles off the podium, cradling them to his chest as he backed away from me. "We're good here. You passed this iteration. Go join your class."

Giving him my sweetest, "butter wouldn't melt in my mouth" smile, I said, "Thank you so much. I think this lesson has been *super* instructive. Don't you?" I tossed my braid off my shoulder and turned to leave. "You have a nice day now."

But as good as it felt to scare the shit out of Ames, I just couldn't enjoy it too much.

Two hours of lecture later, I was pretty sure I was one inane comment away from screaming. This particular iteration involved recognizing and concocting witch circles, sigils, antidotes, and sleeping potions. As someone who had researched all said items explicitly so

I could *avoid* them, I was leaps and bounds ahead of my non-witch classmates.

"Take a break, everyone. Meet back here after lunch," Instructor Haynes announced. "Then we'll be performing practical applications of general antidotes and sleeping potions."

Haynes was a tall, gangly fellow with sunset-pink hair and dark-brown skin. A witch by nature, he seemed nice enough, but he was teaching a crowd of non-witches. The majority of the class were mages, ghouls, shifters, and psychics, and other than Malia, I was the only other sort-of witch here.

Fiona should be here, too, but she wasn't, and the sheer amount of rage at that fact, roiled in my gut.

"I don't know how I'm going to remember all of that," Hannah muttered, pinching her brow. "I feel like my brain is going to explode."

"Don't worry about it," Malia replied, stacking a paperback copy of the Proctor grimoire on top of her legal pad full of notes. "Your main concern is the sigils and circles. No one but a witch will be making potions, anyway, and those all have recipes."

I nodded. "If my two hundred- and fifty-year-old grandmother still needs to look at the book, no one is going to make you go without."

But I didn't give a shit about any of it. I wanted to

know what they thought about Girard's pronounce-ment and if they believed him. And it wasn't until we heard Benjamin and Cole hissing back and forth outside of the dining hall did a spark of hope hit me.

"There's no way. Did you see how she was kicking ass yesterday? She had better grades than all of us, and then she up and quits? Bullshit, man." Benjamin ran a hand through his purple hair, tugging on the ends like he'd really enjoy ripping it out and starting over.

Hallelujah and a-fucking-men. At least someone was thinking the same as me.

"My brother's friend came through here two years ago, and they had something similar happen. A girl 'quit,'" Cole replied, using air quotes and everything. "But she left everything behind. Her clothes, her shoes, everything. They never saw her again. And where the fuck are all the female instructors? That seems a little off, man. Eight female candidates and *no* female instructors?"

My stomach gave an indelicate rumble as I diverted in their direction. But Fiona was more important than my hunger. "Thank the gods. I'm so glad someone else doesn't believe it, either."

Malia and Hannah nodded in agreement, just as worried as I was.

They knew just how determined Fiona was to do

something on her own without her family involved. She wanted something for herself, and it was a common thread that we shared—the need to be something other than our last name.

"No way. Fi? Leave? She'd rather give up her entire shoe collection than pass up a way to stick it to her dad. And that girl has a fuck of a lot of shoes." Benjamin yanked on his hair again, his agitation making his fingers shake.

"Exactly," Hannah rumbled. "And she isn't the first girl to leave. Something funny is going on here."

Another girl from the other cabin joined our little group. Georgia? Gwendolyn? I couldn't remember her name. She didn't talk much and didn't seem to hang with the other girls in her cabin.

"Youse guys talkin' about Fiona?" she asked in a heavy Northern accent. New York or Boston, maybe? "I gotta tell ya, I'm worried. That girl is sweet as pie. No way she'd make us all worry about her like this. She woulda told someone she was leavin' this hellhole. No question about it."

I was ecstatic that I wasn't the only one to think something was up.

"Plus, my cousin gave me the skinny on that Ames jerkoff. She warned me about him. Said somethin' funny was goin' on that only started when he got here a coupla years ago. Female instructors started leavin' and students just up and went *poof*." She looked right at me. "And he seems to have a beef with you, doll. Gotta say, I ain't feeling so warm and fuzzy about this place."

She wasn't the only one.

By the time we'd made it back to class, I'd actually learned the girl's name—Gianna—and now knew she was an Osprey shifter from Brooklyn. She also came from a big ABI family. Her parents, cousins, brothers, and her grandparents had been or were still agents. I'd never met a bird shifter before, but it did explain a decent number of her mannerisms and her bright-gold eyes that were more yellow than anything else.

"I want you to split into partners and work together to create the general poison antidote found on page forty-two," Haynes instructed, handing out metal cauldrons. "Once that is done, I want you to work together to find the ten sigils around the room."

With Fiona gone, there was an odd number of students. I supposed being by myself was probably safer, anyway. Trudging to the front, I was last in line for a cauldron. Haynes handed me one with a gentle smile, and I took it with a worried one of my own.

"This is just... These antidotes aren't meant to work, right? I know I'm the only witch here, but," I leaned in, whispering, "I don't really have any magic. I can mix the ingredients all day but the magic ain't there if you know what I mean."

Haynes' eyebrows shot up to his forehead. "You're an uninherit?"

Wincing, I contemplated his words. An uninherit was exactly that—an arcaner that was born without any magic at all. Some lived to be ancient, some died a human's death. I was somewhere outside of that scope.

"Sure. We'll go with that."

Haynes' gaze narrowed. "A Bannister uninherit? Your grandmama must have had kittens when she found out. No wonder."

Shrugging, I nodded, not quite understanding what he meant. "I guess?"

Haynes rose from the side of his desk, flicking back his curl of pink hair. "Oh, honey, don't worry about a thing. I only want to make sure you can follow directions. Not all of us are like Ames, you know."

With that reassurance, I went back to my table and started the process. Antidotes required a hot cauldron, the right ingredients, and patience—or at least that was what I remembered my grandmother saying a very long time ago in one of my earliest memories.

The instructions called for a poultice to go over a poisoned wound and a tincture to activate the mixture. Quickly, I got to work, mixing the ingredients like it was damn cake and trying not to think about anything other than what I was doing.

Okay, that was a lie.

I was obsessing over the fact that I could mix the damn things together without blowing everything and every*one* to smithereens, Fiona, the delicious night with Nico, and wondering if I could poison Ames and not get in trouble. That was until I felt eyes on me. Looking up, my gaze went right to the window and a pair of golden eyes glowing in the distant tree line.

Last night when I noticed them staring at me in the forest, I'd been scared out of my mind. Now? I was doing my level best to not grin like an idiot while I stirred the poultice together in my mortar. For the first time since I'd left him, I felt semi-okay. Though, maybe he was just trying to keep me from burning the place to the ground, but I was sort of fine with that.

"That's perfect, Wren," Haynes murmured, staring at my mortar, and solidly breaking me out of my Nico spiral. "And the tincture?"

Shakily, I held out the glass vial filled with greenish liquid. Tinctures were usually alcohol-based and smelled to high heaven, but from what I heard, they worked. Haynes studied the bottle through a crystal monocle with sacred geometry etched into the glass.

He pulled the glass from his face. "You sure you're an uninherit?"

Wide-eyed, I stared at the tincture like it might explode. "I didn't say that. I said I couldn't do magic."

Haynes nodded, putting the monocle to his eye again. "Interesting. At first glance, the concoction seems completely without arcane residue, but... if you turn it to the light just like this and..."

Suddenly, Haynes' eyeglass cracked, as did the tincture bottle. He pulled it from his face, examining the crystal as if he'd never seen it before. "Interesting."

Cringing, I wrung my hands. "Did I fail?"

The instructor observed me with an enigmatic smile. "No, you did everything perfectly. Why don't you pick out the sigils hidden in the room, and I—"

"I already found them." I'd picked out the markings on my first visit to this room this afternoon after my foray with Ames. They were etched into the walls, hidden behind random objects, and even in the floor.

"All ten?" Haynes raised his eyebrows.

"There are twenty-three active ones and two inactive ones, but only if you count the etched circle under the desks that nullifies the no-magic wards. It's so weird a null on a null." It was why I'd given that particular circle a wide berth. The last thing I needed was to cross the damn thing while wearing this necklace.

Haynes' eyes went wide as his face paled. "Ah. Umm, anyone ever tell you you're a prodigy? Or call you blessed?"

My snort was indelicate but totally warranted. "No. I cannot recall any member of my family saying anything of the sort. The only person who calls me 'blessed' is Ames, and I don't think he means it in a good way."

Haynes seemed to take that in stride. "Fair enough. You have completed today's iteration and have passed with flying colors. You may go back to your cabin or..." He trailed off, staring through the window to the tree line. "Or maybe get dinner. Good work, Bannister."

I couldn't count how many times I'd been scolded or torn down in my life, but I could count the times I'd been complimented. Swallowing hard, I tried not to start bawling.

"Thanks," I croaked, proud for some reason. Okay, so I knew why. I'd stood up to Ames. I'd done a simple tincture and poultice without blowing up the room. I was on a roll.

Maybe I could really do this.

Gathering my things, I left the classroom, cringing a little when I saw Malia and Hannah's tincture. For one, it was bright purple, and two? The poultice was bubbling over the mortar. I was one thousand percent certain neither of those things should have happened.

The crisp mountain air hit my nose as the null ward closed in around me. But one thing stood out over the scent of oak and pine. Nico's scent was on the air—something I wouldn't have smelled before last night. He was in those woods somewhere, waiting. Watching. But it felt like a warm blanket, hugging me, protecting me against the cold.

But even though I felt his presence all around me, he never came out of the shadows, and I didn't see him as I went back to my empty cabin. The place was cold without Fiona, her bubbly nature livening the place. Without her, it was just a rickety cabin with metal wall lockers and a shabby exterior.

The last time I'd been in here, Nico had such an odd look on his face—like he'd expected me not to come walking in. It had been that same look on his face last night in the woods when I'd really been leaving.

And when he stopped waiting and finally came through that door, I didn't know who ran to who first.

CHAPTER 15

NICO

Twelve hours.

Twelve fucking hours.

I'd counted them like years while I waited and watched and made sure Wren was safe. There was something going on here, and I'd been so stupid not to see it before. The worst part? If Wren hadn't been in my cabin last night, she could have been the one taken.

That thought always came back and bit me when I was least expecting it. As I roamed the woods trying to catch Jacobs' scent, as I tried to get a hint of that girl anywhere on the grounds. But it was if someone had erased her completely.

Because that was the rub, wasn't it? If Jacobs had gone of her own accord, she would have taken her things. She would have left a trail I could follow to the front gate. She would have said goodbye. Her situation was nothing like Wren's.

Jacobs didn't have to leave in the middle of the night without a word.

But she did.

She did, and there wasn't a single trace of her anywhere. The only place her scent remained was on a square of pillow. Not on her clothes, not in her obviously used bedsheets.

Nothing.

To me that meant spell work—high-level spell work at that. There were only a handful of arcaners I knew of who could cast under a null and live to tell the tale. And none of them I wanted anywhere near Wren. I had to get her the hell out of here. It wasn't safe for her anymore—if it had ever been.

A part of me hated myself for making her stay, for letting my wolf bind us when she was so vulnerable. What a fool I had been for keeping her here, but finding a way out now that wouldn't put her neck on the chopping block...

Well, I didn't know if there was one.

The sensation of her waiting was killing me. It was a weight, a living thing, and keeping away from her was so much worse now that I'd marked her that I wasn't sure if I was sane anymore. It had never made sense to me, the crazed need for one's mate, but now I knew.

I knew and it was awful.

My feet pointed themselves to Wren's door, moving faster and faster until I was no longer on four paws but two, racing for that damn cabin like I would die if I didn't. I'd meant to be smooth, to act like the adult I was, but twelve fucking hours of absence, one missing girl, and her scent so close?

I was done for.

In the back of my mind, I knew she was alone. I knew it was safe to be there, and I was glad for that, because as soon as I opened that damn door that divided us, Wren was running, racing for me, too. I caught her on a jump, her arms and legs wrapping around me as mine closed around her in a gripping embrace. Then her mouth was on mine, the sweetness of her tongue dancing with my own, making the world fall away for a moment.

Naturally, her back found the closest wall, the press of her body against me, bringing a peace I thought was fleeting. Her finger scraped my scalp, and I fought the urge to rip her clothes right off here and sink into the blissful warmth between her thighs. Unfortunately, there was the matter of Wren's cabinmates and the fact I should not be in here at all.

Ghoul noses weren't easy to fool. If we gave into ripping off each other's clothes, our cover would be blown.

Somehow, I wrestled some blood back to the big brain and managed to break the kiss. Wren's breaths came in shuddering little pants, and that was nearly enough to drive me over the edge.

Mate.

Gritting my teeth, I set her down, but was unable to move away.

Her smile was half-lust and half complete innocence. "Good evening, Instructor Acosta. Is there something I can help you with?"

Why, that little shit.

Fitting my hand under her braid, I cupped the back of her neck as I bent down to whisper in her ear. "There are many things you can help me with, beautiful, but I do recall telling you to call me Nico when we were together. Maybe I'll tie you up and make you come over and over until you remember."

Her shiver was absolutely priceless, as was the scent of her arousal. If I could have that burned into my brain for the rest of my life, I'd live a very happy man.

"Is that supposed to be a threat?" she said breathlessly. "Because if it is, you should really work on your intimidation skills."

I wanted to stay right here—this banter, this bubble of happiness—but it wouldn't last. Not here.

"Grab what you need for the night. You're staying with me."

Frowning, Wren pushed at my belly. "No, I'm not." She gestured to Jacobs' empty bed. "Someone came into this cabin and took my friend, Nico. I don't know if you believe Girard or not, but I don't. No way am I going to leave Hannah and Malia to the same damn fate. What if..."

She grimaced, shaking her head. "What if I could have stopped it? What if I could have helped her? And now, I don't know where she is. I don't know if she's alive. Girard lied to my face. I know he did. And I—"

Gently, I put my hand over her mouth and a single finger to mine. "I believe you," I breathed, my voice barely audible to even my ears. "Pack a bag. A small one. You're coming back."

Yeah, she was going back, and I would be in wolf form, watching her cabin all night long and praying no one got by me. I'd already left five messages for Wyatt to get his ass back here. I needed backup—and yesterday.

Wren seemed to think about it for a minute, likely debating her loyalty to her friends over finding out whatever it was I had to say. Her curiosity won.

"Fine," she mouthed, snatching her empty bright-purple duffle from under her bed, and stuffing a few things into it.

Shit she absolutely would not need. Like pajamas. And underwear.

In a matter of seconds, we were out of her cabin and picking through the trees to mine, sometimes filtering deeper into the forest to avoid the students returning from class. And all the while, my wolf was nearly silent because I had her hand in mine, bringing her back to my den.

Den? Gods, I'm going full-on wolf now.

As soon as I got us back to the safety of my space, I did what I'd wanted to do all fucking day. I wrapped my arms around her and breathed her in. I'd been on edge since I'd left her, and now? Now, I was almost okay.

Almost.

"Do you think she's dead?" Wren croaked, holding me tight to her as she buried her face in my chest.

I didn't know how to answer that. Could Jacobs be dead? Of course she could. But something told me she wasn't. Something told me none of the women gone were dead, and personally, I didn't think that was a good thing.

"No, beautiful. I think your friend is a fighter."

Wren lifted her head. "You think someone took her, too, right?"

Grimly, I nodded. Pivoting on a heel, I headed for the small kitchenette, needing a beer for this conversation. Popping the top off a bottle, I took a huge swig before offering Wren one of her own.

A little green, she shook her head. "No thank you. I'm swearing off booze until I can look at it without wanting to vomit."

I tried and failed not to smile at her aversion to alcohol. It was a shining spot in the absolute fuck-shit we needed to go over. Returning the beer, I selected a bottle of water and handed it over.

"A week ago, a good friend of mine asked me to come here to nose around. Over the last few years, female instructors have been consistently putting in for transfers or quitting the ABI altogether. So much so, there isn't a single one left at this post. Similarly, more than a handful of female students have also voided their contracts. Since the paperwork is fine, no one bats an eye, so it's tough to prove something is going on. I could easily brush this off, except..."

Wren jumped up on the counter, the same counter that I'd almost kissed her on what seemed like forever ago. "Except?"

"Except... I snooped around your friend's area, trying to catch a scent so I could follow her trail.

Problem is? There isn't one. Not on her bedclothes or her shoes or her makeup bag. Not one scent."

She leaned forward, fitting her elbows onto her knees. "But you're a wolf. That's not possible. You would at least get the scent of the fabric or the products. You'd smell the leather of her shoes or the chemicals in her makeup. You'd get something. So that means someone spelled her things."

If there had ever been a doubt that Wren was a smart cookie, it was gone now.

"So, what do we do?" she asked, jumping off the counter. "Do we call in the cavalry? Get some agents here or—"

"We can't," I said, cutting her off. I hated to do it, but I didn't want her hope to grow. "We don't have a shred of evidence, other than me *not* smelling something. I can't exactly go to my supervisor with that."

Wren's face quickly changed from pale to pink to fire-engine red, her fists balling at her sides. "So, we do nothing?"

"I didn't say th—"

"No." She cut me off. "You said we can't call anyone. Even though there's enough rumors floating around that every single trainee is talking about girls going missing. That they see there aren't any female instructors, and they think it's weird as fuck. That people are scared they're going to be next. Sure, Nico. Now's not the time to call anyone. All because you don't have more. It's enough for an inquiry at the very least." Two steps and she was in my face, stabbing her index finger into my chest. "Bare minimum, call her family. Hell, call anyone's family. Call the agent's next duty station. Ask if they ever showed up. Ask if you can talk to them. Ask literally anything."

It was tough not to start smiling. My mate was smart and loyal and damn near rabid when it came to protecting those she held dear. I fucking loved it.

"Wyatt—my friend—already tried," I murmured, grabbing her hand, and kissing the back of it. "He couldn't get access to the files. I tried, too, when I got here. The only ones I had access to were current students. I looked a few hours ago—Fiona's file is gone."

Tears welled in her eyes as she clenched her teeth. "Shit. I'm sorry. I shouldn't have assumed."

It wasn't exactly a stretch to figure out why she wouldn't want Fiona forgotten. Wren's family had done damn near everything they could to forget my lovely mate even existed. If the same fate had befallen her, I doubted they'd do more than shrug and say, "Good riddance."

They had no idea just how fucking phenomenal she was. How special.

"I won't forget her, Wren, but keeping you safe is a bigger priority to me."

Just admitting that out loud was risky. I'd grown to trust Wren, grown to feel something more for her. I'd accepted that she was my mate over all others, giving her my mark and...

But unlike me, she could leave. She could find someone else. She could choose another.

And I never would.

Wren's confusion made me want to walk up to her father one day and just knock his fucking head off. *How does a man stand idly by while their family shits on their little girl? How does he not fight for her every day?*

"Priority? But she's the one who's missing. I'm jus—"

"Really fucking important to me," I murmured, cutting her off. "What happened to her will not happen to you. You will be safe, and you will graduate this absolute farce of a course, and then we'll go back to Savannah where we fucking well belong."

Her confusion was sweeter this time. "You don't normally work here, do you?"

Clutching her to me, I shook my head. "Nope."

"You're from Savannah."

"Yep," I said, fitting my palms under her thighs and lifting her onto the counter. The last time she'd been up there, I'd wanted to spread her legs wide and taste her. "Born and raised."

Fitting myself between those glorious thighs, I cupped her cheeks in my hands, loving the flare of desire in her eyes as her lips parted.

"I wanted you to kiss me the last time I was up here," she whispered, staring at my lips.

"Funny, all I'd wanted to do was spread you on this counter and fuck that pretty pussy with my tongue." Bringing my mouth to hers, I devoured her moans as I kissed her senseless. "Consider this a do-over."

Dealing with the button on her jeans, we worked together to wiggle the denim down her hips. As more and more of her pale skin was exposed, I dropped wet, biting kisses to her flesh. She tasted fucking divine, that honey scent only getting stronger between her legs. It took work getting her naked, her boots an actual problem—especially with the limited blood flow heading to my brain.

Before I couldn't fight the urge to rip the damn things off her with my claws, I managed to get her naked from the waist down, her perfect pale ass kissing the counter. Needing her bare, we worked off her shirt and bra, and I got the pleasure of raking my fangs over one pert nipple, sucking it into my mouth as I yanked her ass to the edge.

Wren moaned, shaking with need as she clawed at my shirt. Kneeling, I fit my upper body between her knees, tossing her legs over my shoulders as I admired her slick wet sex with its tuft of auburn curls and perfect pink lips.

And her scent? Fuck, I was a goner.

Mine. Mate. Mine.

"Be a good girl and put your hands on the counter, sweetheart," I ordered, the command only making her wetter. She shuddered, her brilliant green-gold eyes practically lighting with challenge.

"What happens if I don't?" she asked, her hips betraying her by swiveling for a little friction.

My teeth found the inside of her thigh, and I raked my fangs against the sensitive flesh. She shuddered in answer, a moan slipping past her lips.

"So many things. I could spank that luscious ass of yours while I fuck it." She bit her lip at that one, and it gave me so many ideas, but I continued. "I could tease you until you beg me to come. I could tie them behind your back and make you." Another lip bite. Oh, I liked that. "Really, the options are limitless, but all of them delay my meal, beautiful, and I'm fucking starving."

Wren slapped her hands on the tile, and fuck, if that wasn't sexy, too.

Spreading her wide with my thumbs, I gave her sweet lips a long lick. It wasn't the first time I'd gotten my mouth on her pussy, but Wren was becoming my favorite treat. Before long I was devouring her, circling my tongue over her clit, pressing my fingers into her. Moans spilled from her throat, husky ones that made my cock harder than a rock and had my balls reaching up my throat.

"Shh, beautiful," I murmured before getting right back to work.

A shaking hand found my free wrist, pulling it from her folds. She then took those fingers and wrapped her lips around them, sucking on the digits like she had my cock last night.

Gods, this woman.

My cock—which had been harder than I thought possible—kicked against my zipper—making anything but taking her impossible. Finding my feet, I pulled my fingers from her mouth, unable to stop myself from kissing her. I wanted her taste on my tongue—all of it. And it just went on and on.

Together, our fingers worked my belt loose, and in far more time than either of us wanted, I was free of my pants. But as impatient as I was, I had nothing on Wren.

"Please," she begged, clawing at my shirt, only this time, the fabric tore under her ministrations. "I want you. *Please*."

Far be it from me to deny my mate anything.

"Since you asked so nicely," I murmured against her lips, swallowing her moan as I pressed inside her wet heat.

Gods, she was Heaven. She was Heaven and Hell, the cosmos and everything in between. Her breath hitched as her eyes glowed with pleasure, her chest and cheeks flushed as her legs tightened around my back. Wren's release was coming fast, and I was right there with her. Lost in her passion, she bared her neck to me, unable to hold her head up a single second longer.

Her braid shifted, revealing the two crescents of my mark on her flesh, the sight making me feral. My thrusts got rougher, harder, her moans louder, and I struck, re-marking her as I had several times last night, ensuring my bite took, cementing us together again and again.

As soon as my fangs broke her skin, her sex tightened around me, her moans getting louder, more desperate. She was almost there. *Almost.* Fitting a hand between us, I circled her clit with my thumb, and she went off like a bomb, triggering a chain reaction of my own climax.

Heat raced up my spine as it overtook me, the last thread of control snapping as I pounded out my release.

I would never be able to look at this counter again without getting hard.

Never.

By the time the moon was high in the sky, we'd come together several more times, exhaustion pulling us into a deep sleep.

Maybe that was why I didn't hear the man's approach until he was already knocking on my door, until he was already too close for comfort. And I had a sleeping Wren in my bed.

A sleeping, naked Wren.

Who was most definitely not supposed to be here.

Fuck.

CHAPTER 16
WREN

The sleep after Nico fucked me into a stupor was the absolute best. It didn't matter if it was five minutes or two hours, it was the most restful sleep I'd ever gotten in my life. Maybe I felt safe with him. And why wouldn't I? In the circle of his arms, nothing could happen to me. No one would get to me. I was special and whole and cared for. Or maybe he screwed me so good, I was incapable of thinking bad thoughts. Whatever it was, his penis should be classified as a deadly weapon.

One good dicking and I was down for the count until he found me again in the night, his hands urgent, needy, and I was fully awake, ready for the next round. There was no way this kind of pace was sustainable, but so far, I wasn't sore, I didn't have any regrets, and my lust wasn't going to die down anytime soon.

But this time when his hands shook me awake, I knew something was wrong. For one, his palm clamped hard over my mouth, pressing my lips against my teeth, and two? He led a finger to his own lips, begging for me to be quiet with his eyes. Unease filtered through my lethargic limbs, the sex-haze lifting as adrenaline kicked in. Then I heard it.

A knock. Someone was at the door. And I was naked in Nico's bed.

Shiiiiittttttttt.

Wrapping me up in a sheet, he picked me up and lowered me to the floor, sliding me on the fabric until I was under the bed, the scant space tight, but I fit. Then he flicked the comforter over the side, hiding me from view.

Shuffling commenced, the rustle of clothes, I think, and then Nico opened his door.

"Girard?" Nico said, his voice the picture of surprise and innocence. "Is something wrong?"

"No, no, Acosta. Nothing's wrong, exactly. It's just... May I come in?"

My blood went cold. If there was a man I didn't trust, it was Girard. At least Ames was up front about his assholery. Girard was stealth about it, keeping his shit hidden until you were blindsided by it. I'd almost thought he was a good guy until he lied right to my face about Fiona. Thought he was better than the Ameses of the world.

But he was no different, except that he was the one wearing a mask.

"Sure," Nico answered, and I wanted to kick him.

Here I was lying naked, wrapped in a sheet on this dust-bunny hell of a floor, trying not to sneeze my head off, and he was inviting him in? Was he high?

The clomp of booted feet tramped into his cabin, and I tried not to pop out from under this bed and slap the shit out of the wolf.

"To what do I owe this pleasure?" Nico prompted, his feigned innocence on thick. The place probably smelled like sex, and I was one thousand percent positive we were going to get made.

A flutter of paper rustled, and Girard replied, "Apologies, I've been on the phone with Savannah for two hours trying to stop this, but you've been recalled."

Recalled? What the fuck did that mean?

"Now? In the middle of a class? I'm supposed to be covering for Cassidy until June. What gives?"

Nico plopped onto the bed, sending the mattress squeezing through the slats, closer to my face. The only thing that ensured it was him was the sliver of bare feet

I could see past the comforter. The man even had pretty feet. How the hell was that possible, and oh, my gods, why was I thinking about his feet at a time like this?

Then it hit me. He was protecting me again, making sure Girard didn't come any closer. Still.

Recalled?

"That's what I said, but the brass isn't having it. They want you there first thing in the morning."

That cold pit of dread? Well, it was a certified iceberg now.

He was leaving? Now?

How were we going to find out what happened to Fiona? What about Ames? If Nico was gone, Ames would run roughshod over everyone. And I didn't trust Girard as far as I could throw him.

He was leaving. He was leaving me.

Me. Us. He could find anyone. Nico Acosta was a virile, hot-as-sin wolf with so much goodness in him it made my heart want to burst out of my chest. He didn't have to be stuck with someone like me, a fuckup who couldn't even do magic. A witch so messed up, even her own family didn't want her. Nico could have anyone he wanted. No doubt there were arcaners and humans alike, just throwing themselves at his feet while he walked down the street. It was a wonder he could get anything done at all.

He was leaving.

Tears welled in my stupid eyes as my chest wanted to cave in on itself. My throat hurt and my heart... This was just some fling. He could go back to his life and forget all about me—about this place. He could move on and not grasp at the straws of a mystery that no one had gotten anywhere on in years. He could be free.

A small place at the back of my mind wanted that for him. Happiness. Freedom. A life without worry, or a stupid girl clinging to him that was more trouble than she was worth.

Self-esteem needed on aisle three. We need some self-esteem over here.

Yeah, I was a self-deprecating, no-magic-having witch with abandonment issues, but that didn't change the facts. Nico would leave, and I would be here, and surviving would become a problem.

Fiona.

How was I going to find her now? By myself, I guessed. Because I wouldn't leave her behind.

I wouldn't.

Because the reality was, that if I had really left, no one but her would give a shit. She'd do whatever it was she had to do to find me. It was only fitting I do the same.

"Why didn't my supervisor contact me?" Nico countered, his tone conversational but probing. "This is pretty fucking irregular, man."

I wiped at my face, dashing the wetness from my cheeks, and swallowing down the rest of my tears. Tears never did help anybody, right? What good were they when I had shit to do?

Find Fiona. The rest of this shit doesn't matter. Your heart, your feelings? They mean shit.

"No idea. Check your phone. Maybe they tried."

Nico sighed. "I'll do that. Sorry to leave you in the lurch, Girard. Hopefully, Cassidy is already on his way back, so you don't have a hole in the schedule."

He was leaving.

Yes. He was. And as much as that shit hurt, as much as it frightened me with everything going on, as much as I would miss him, I had to get on with it. Get on with living without him. He'd be doing the same damn thing without me.

No pity parties. No moping. No crying myself to sleep. Nothing. I would be fine. I always was.

I always fucking am.

"Here's hoping," Girard replied, his booted feet plodding toward the door. "Sorry about the rush. Hope everything's okay in Savannah."

"Yeah," Nico said, rising from the bed. "Thanks, man."

The door opened and shut, and by the time Nico pulled the comforter back to tell me the coast was clear, I'd already dried my tears and concocted a plan. This one was slightly better than the one I'd come up with while cleaning the dining hall, but not by much.

You're fine. You always are. Just swallow it down and smile like the good girl you are and don't make a fuss. No one likes a fuss, Wren.

How many times had my mother said that?

No one likes a fuss, Wren.

Smile, girl. Gods, you got cotton for brains?

Can't you go over to your little friend's house so we can have some damn peace around here?

Don't make a fuss. Mama was right about that.

Nico held out a hand, and as much as it hurt, I took it, allowing him to pull me from the floor and into his arms, gritting my teeth all the while. His scent surrounded me, as did his heat—a warmth I'd only found right here against his chest. I never realized how cold I'd been for all these years—not until he held me.

He's leaving, and he's not coming back. This is goodbye.

His fingers burrowed into my hair, his blunted nails gently scratching at my scalp. It felt so good, and it hurt so bad all at the same time. Then he kissed my temple, my cheek, my neck, wrapping me up so tight, I almost believed he didn't want to go.

Almost.

I wanted to bawl. I wanted to rage. I wanted to tie him down and make sure he never left. But I didn't do any of those things. One by one, I closed every door and window into my heart, locking them up tight.

No more. I wouldn't give any more of me. Not one more bit.

I had to save something for myself. I had to make it so I could breathe, could live. I wasn't going to give more of myself than I could survive losing, and I would give him everything if I let myself.

As gently as I could, I pushed against his middle, aching for space, for an ounce of distance. He couldn't hug me and kiss me and make me think he wanted me —not when he was leaving me behind. Turning, I searched for my clothes and boots, my bag, anything, but the small cabin was cleared of my things. As if I'd never been here.

Nodding, that ache only got bigger. It was as it should be.

"Oh, here," he murmured, sensing my distress and went to a teeny closet. He pulled my bag and discarded clothes from the floor, handing them over.

I croaked out a quiet, "Thanks," before heading to the bathroom to shower and handle my business, the worst sense of déjà vu coming over me. Hadn't I done this yesterday? Hurt my own feelings and fled to the bathroom to shower off his scent? Hadn't I needed that space?

The water felt like needles against my skin, but I scrubbed him from me, every kiss, every scent, every hug—soaping them over and washing them down the drain. My skin was raw by the time I quit, but again, it didn't matter. None of it mattered.

Then I was out of the bathroom just in time to see Nico zip a bag of his own. It was a little larger than mine, bright yellow, and it sat on top of our wadded-up sheets.

"Come on, beautiful. Let me get you back to your cabin safe, and I—"

"Don't worry about it. I can make it there on my own." I couldn't take one more kiss. Or hug. Or bullshit promise he knew he couldn't keep—that I knew he wouldn't keep. Giving him my best "I'm not broken" smile, I softened it with, "You need to go, right?"

Nico's gaze went gold, glowing with his wolf. "I don't want to go. You know that, right?"

Sure I did.

"Of course," I murmured, shouldering my bag. "I understand."

His fingers wrapped around my wrist, a gentle

handcuff if there ever was one. "I don't think you do. I don't think you understand any of it."

But there wasn't anything for me not to get, and even though he was barely holding onto me, it hurt so fucking bad, I almost wished his grip was bruising.

"What's not to understand? You've been recalled, you need to go. I got it, Nico. Trust me."

Somehow, in the split second it took me to pivot away from him, he was in my space, my bag was gone, and he had backed me into a wall, my back flat to the planks.

"No," he growled, his chest rumbling against mine. "You don't. You couldn't possibly. Because if you did, you'd get that I would rather eat glass than leave you."

Hope bloomed in my heart. Stupid hope. What had hope ever done for anybody, huh? It broke you, that's what it did. It made you believe things were possible when they never were. It made you think if you just tried hard enough, if you just pushed a little more, if you were better, then people would love you. People would give a shit.

Hope made me a doormat.

But then he cupped my cheeks in his hands and stared at me with those gorgeous gold eyes, and I softened. Just a little.

"If you understood, you'd get that every time you

leave my sight, I get twitchy. I get distracted. All I want to do is get back to you. If you understood, you'd know that I fucking hate that I have to leave. I *hate* it. You'd know that I'm scared out of my fucking mind something is going to happen to you. That I'm freaking the fuck out over here."

Goo. I was goo—puddled on the floor, certified liquid, goo.

"Problem is, if they're recalling me, things have gone sideways, and they need my help. They wouldn't do that—especially with this quick of a turnaround—if shit was copacetic. I need to get there, fix whatever the fuck it is that has them recalling me, and get back before the place explodes, or worse."

I thought about the cracked crystal in Haynes' hand. Blowing shit up was a very real possibility.

"So do you get it now? I don't want to leave, but I have to. I don't want you unprotected, but I don't know another way to keep you safe. And every single second I'm gone, it's going to feel like I cut out my fucking heart."

Rolling up on my tiptoes, I pressed a kiss to his full lips, tasting his words for the truth they were. When we were breathless and rumpled, I said, "Yeah. I was a little unclear, but I get it now. Thanks for the clarification."

"Good," he murmured, letting go of my face and grabbing my hand.

He led me much the same way he'd brought me here, through the forest, dipping through the trees when he heard something I couldn't. In no time we were back at my cabin, walking through the rear door. This time, though, the cabin wasn't empty.

Not at all.

CHAPTER 17
WREN

Nico froze and then backed up three steps, clutching me to his back as he moved, protecting me with his body. His entire form—save for his neck—was as still as a statue. That neck, though? It was tilted up by the point of a silver knife.

Hannah stood in the doorway, her giant ghoul frame of nearly seven feet blocking the entrance, the blade in her steady fist. And she was growling, a deep belly sound that rumbled from the depths of Hell.

Umm, Houston? We have a problem.

"Stand down, Dumond," Nico ordered, threading whatever power he had into the command. "She's right here. Look."

But the whispers around the camp were that

Hannah had survived an almost extinction of her nest—
the *only* survivor—and my green-haired ghoul friend
had no intention of taking her eyes off Nico. Especially
not when he was entering our cabin in the middle of the
night right after Fiona had been taken.

But I'd be damned if Nico got hurt because of me.
Hell no.

A film of red passed over my eyes for a moment
before I barked, "Hannah Dumond, you get that knife
away from his neck right now, or so help me, I will
knock your fucking block off."

Could I knock her block off? Absolutely not.

The best I could do was kick her in the shin and run
for my life, but that wasn't the point. That knife needed
to be nowhere near Nico, and that was just the way it
had to be.

Hannah finally flicked her gaze to me, her eyes going
wide, shock and a fair amount of relief in those impossibly pale irises. In a millisecond, the knife was spirited
away to who knew where and her hand was on my
wrist, yanking me into the cabin with about as much
finesse as a wrecking ball.

Nico seemed to take umbrage with her rough
handling because the sound that came from his throat
scared the shit out of even me. If Hannah's had been

from Hell itself, then Satan or Hades or whoever ran the place was coming out of Nico.

"Lock your shit up, Dumond, you hear me? You don't touch her like that. Ever. Understand?"

It was more order than question, but she got it just fine, letting go of my wrist like it burned her.

"Got it, wolf. Crystal clear."

"Excuse the fuck out of us," Malia chimed in, elbowing Hannah out of the way, "but maybe don't leave your scent and impressions all over the place after one of our friends up and goes missing and then kidnap someone else in this cabin. You think you can do that, you fucking idiot?"

Then she took off her glove and smacked me with it. "And you. You think you can stave off spending the night with your boyfriend for one night maybe? What the fuck? We thought you'd been taken, too, until I touched your locker and found out otherwise. Dick. Move."

I shot Nico a withering glare. "Told you it was a bad idea to leave."

His answering smile told me he did not give that first shit about their discomfort. He did not regret a single second of our time alone.

Okay, I didn't either, but still. We'd been rude, worrying them like that.

"And if you could stop eye-fucking each other for five seconds, that would be great," Malia snapped, making my head whip to her.

Oops.

Nico tucked me under his arm, protecting me, even in this safe space. "How about you stop barking orders at us and agree to watch out for my girl here until I can get back? How'd that be?" His eyes flashed with his wolf, and I hated to say it, but it was really freaking hot. Nico's attention shifted to Hannah. "Not out of your sight for a second. It's going to be a while until I can get a buddy here. Do this favor for me and I'll owe you one."

Hannah crossed her arms over her chest, eyeballing him with derision. "A freebie favor from a wolf prince for doing something I was already going to do?" She shrugged like dropping that bomb was no big deal. "Sure, I'm game."

Wolf prince?

"Wolves don't have royalty like you ghouls, and you're one to talk, *Queen.*"

"Don't fucking call me that," she growled, hers almost as scary as Nico's. "You're lucky she likes you, wolf."

"Yeah, yeah. I'm sufficiently scared," he deadpanned, his bored expression nearly making me giggle.

Giggling? What am I, twelve?

Nico grabbed my hand and lifted my knuckles to his lips. "Nowhere alone, beautiful. Not to the bathroom, no iterations, nothing. Got me? Don't make it harder for her to watch out for you or I'll never hear the end of it."

Rolling my eyes, I fit a hand on my hip. "I'm a girl, Nico. I haven't gone to the bathroom by myself since I got boobs."

He blinked hard at that one but nodded, anyway. "Fair enough."

Then his mouth was on mine, a searing kiss to tide mc over for however long he would be gone.

"Be safe, Wren."

And then he really was gone, slipping out of the cabin as if he'd never been there. Already I felt cold, Nico taking all his warmth with him. Pouting, I plopped onto my bed, very aware of the two women staring at me like I had a second head.

"What?"

Hannah approached, leaning over my bed like a weirdo. "I don't care what soap you used or how much you scrubbed, I can still smell him on you. I would have given you shit about it this morning, but Fiona happened, so I skipped it." She tilted her head, her gaze flitting over the collar of my shirt. "So, you and the wolf, huh? Explain that to me."

Shrugging, I sat up and started unpacking my bag, unsure how to answer her.

"Wish I could, but I can't. It doesn't make a bit of sense to me, either. For some weird reason, he decided I was who he wanted, and..." I trailed off, shaking my head.

"So the sex is combustible. Got it." Hannah nodded like this was the best explanation. I wanted to argue, but she wasn't wrong.

"By the way," Malia chimed in, "everything you touch has Acosta's imprint all over it. Like literally everything. Question: Did he really do that thing with his fingers—"

"Whoa," I shouted, shooting to my feet. "That shit is private, ma'am."

But yes. Yes, he did do that thing with his fingers. And it was fucking divine.

Malia stuck out her tongue. "Don't touch my toothbrush, and I won't glean information I'm not supposed to have."

At that, I laughed—so hard it brought tears to my eyes, but then my mirth took a right turn back into depressed-land. Nico was gone. Fiona was gone. And somehow, we needed to pass this course and not get kidnapped, or killed, or worse.

Piece of cake.

OVER THE NEXT FEW HOURS, WE ALL GOT TOO LITTLE SLEEP, one of us waking up in the middle of the night, afraid of what could happen. At about two, we decided as a group to just leave all the lights on, foregoing sleep entirely.

Fiona had been taken right under all our noses. It could be any of us next.

After an uneasy breakfast, we were in the middle of a necromancy lecture with Girard, going over all the ways the practice was regulated, what was allowed, and why you shouldn't raise the dead willy-nilly.

All while trying to stay awake. Sure, it was inter-esting stuff, but the lecture went on and on. Personally, I figured raising the dead was kind of a no-no on all fronts and any thought to the contrary was absolute insanity. But the arcane world probably didn't give two shits about my opinion on the subject.

And I got it—I did.

Savannah was home to hundreds of cemeteries. Our steps and walls and very foundations were made of arcaner bones. It wasn't like being surrounded by death was exactly new.

But making them come back to life? Full-on zombies?

No, thanks.

I was a criminal. Not an idiot.

After the lecture, there would be an exam—one I would pass, because the answer to everything was basically, "do not raise the dead, don't think about raising the dead, don't talk about raising the dead, and don't be friends with people who raise the dead." It was basically a no-brainer.

Sure enough, when the test was delivered, it was a poster lesson for "do not do the thing" and if you "do the thing," you would go to jail while you awaited your very swift execution.

So noted.

But as I was finishing my test, I dragged my feet a little, my original plan bubbling in my head. Girard was lying to all of us. Nico couldn't get a scent off of her things. Someone had to have enough juice to do magic under the null ward.

Who better to have that level of magic than the commandant of the damn course? All the fingers pointed to Ames, but no way he was smart enough or had enough clout to fake the paperwork needed to keep this shit quiet.

But Girard did.

And if he was a creepy arcane serial killer, he'd have to keep trophies, right? I watched enough true crime shows to know all serial killers liked trophies. What if he had them? What if they were just sitting in his office? What if I could get the proof Nico needed to take this asshole down?

I looked it up. The ABI didn't require search warrants or Miranda rights. They didn't need permission—mostly because if they had a shred of proof you did something, they'd take your ass to jail posthaste.

So, any trial Girard had, it wouldn't get thrown out because I'd nicked some evidence.

And I wouldn't get a more perfect time to search, either. Girard was proctoring this test, and no one had finished yet. I had plenty of time to get in, search, and get out.

This is the dumbest idea you have ever had in your life, Wren, and that's saying something.

Okay, my inner voice—who still sounded like my mother—was accurate. This was stupid. But Nico was gone, and his friend was nowhere to be found, and who the fuck was going to look for Fiona while we sat here with our thumbs up our asses?

No one. That's who.

Shoring up my topsy-turvy nerves, I stood, taking my test right to the front and handing it in.

Girard's eyes sparkled, a warm smile on his face like he was a proud papa. It made me sick.

"Already, Bannister?" His gaze traced over the page as if he was mentally grading it on the spot. "Very good. You're free to enjoy some leisure time until your next iteration."

Pasting my best smile on my face, I shoved out a polite, "Thank you," before pivoting on a heel and marching through the aisle of desks to leave. But as I walked past Hannah's desk, she flung out a hand to stop me.

She didn't say anything. She didn't need to. Everything in her gaze said to go straight back to our cabin with no stops, and whatever it was that I was planning had better not happen.

I nodded, only to be answered by her narrowed eyes.

It was funny how well you could get to know someone so fast. Our silent conversation went a little like this:

Her: *No funny business.*

Me: *I'm not doing anything.*

Her: *Bullshit. I'm watching you.*

Me: *Fine.*

"Is there something wrong?" Girard asked, standing at his desk.

"No, sir," I called, pulling my wrist from Hannah's vise-grip of a hand. "Just leaving."

Then I was out the door, praying no one got wise for a little while.

The first problem I ran into was finding Girard's office. I vaguely remembered the map from the first day, which pointed out the medical cabin and surrounding offices. After Hell Night, I'd avoided the place like the plague, the lack of a null sort of a problem for someone like me.

But now I had a nulling necklace...

And even though Haynes' crystal had cracked, maybe the thing had enough juice to get me in and out of there without being detected. Directing my feet north, I stuck to the trees, skirting the buildings until I came to the medic cabin. Next to the cute cottage-style bungalow was another, recessed back into the trees as if it were hiding.

If I was a creepy whatever the fuck Girard was, I'd want an office tucked away, almost hidden from all the students.

Sure, and how are you getting in there? And what happens if this isn't the place? What if someone is in the building?

Okay, so my plan was "absolute flying by the seat of my pants, dumbest shit ever, why are you like this," bad.

I should turn around and never come back, just keep my head down and get through the course and pray someone else got the balls to find Fiona.

Wren, there are far more people that care about you than you think.

Fiona's words hit me like a slap. She wouldn't chicken out on me. She would have found something. I was sure of it.

Gritting my teeth, I pressed forward. Smartly—one of the few smart moves I'd had all damn day—I circled the building, listening for voices or movement. With human-capable ears, I didn't get anything, and I prayed that was enough. Like most of the other cabins, there was a back door, and I tested the knob.

Much to my disbelief, the door was unlocked, and I walked inside, keeping an eye out for something or someone to jump out at me. The cabin was larger than Nico's, the main area divided into rooms instead of wide open. The back opened into a mud and laundry room with three pairs of soiled boots, all the same size. On the hooks were a few jackets in different weights and a stand-up washer-dryer combo.

From there, was a larger kitchen with new appliances and stone countertops that led into a decent living room, with a large television and standard bachelor-pad-style leather recliners. Across from the living room was a bedroom with a messy comforter and an office close to the front door.

This was Girard's home.

Somehow being in Girard's house seemed like way worse of an idea than his office ever was.

You should not be here, Wren.

Yeah, yeah, I knew that. But I was here already, and my time was running out.

Bolting for the office, I drew up short. For one, the place was an absolute mess. Papers were strewn all over the floor, the computer monitor on its side, the screen cracked. Blood dotted the white copy paper, blending into the black ink.

You should not be here, Wren.

Seeing the blood, the office, I finally decided my inner voice was right.

But before I could even turn to leave, a sharp pain tore through my skull, and everything went black.

"Where the fuck have you been?" I barked, not taking my eyes off the road. There was little traffic this late at night, but not paying attention was a good way to ram right into a deer.

Wyatt was on the line, filtering through my truck's speakers, his chuckle dark. He was lucky he wasn't in this damn cab with me. I'd called that man no less than ten times, trying to get his ass back to the selection school, and now two hours into the drive down to Savannah, he was calling me back?

About fucking time.

"Cleaning up messes, man. Cleaning up a shit-ton of messes and making a few of my own. I got your messages. All ten of them. It's why I'm calling."

Pressing the accelerator, I ground my teeth, trying not to yell. "Fabulous. We'll talk about your messes later. I need you back at the school. Now."

Wyatt sucked air between his teeth. "That's a tall order, my friend. I'm not exactly in a spot where I can just leave."

"She's unprotected, Wyatt. One girl has already been taken, and Wren is there without me. She is my mate, my *wife*. And because of my obligation to the ABI, I'm now driving away from her. So I need you to get to a spot where you can leave, and need you to do it now."

"Ho-ly shit. Really? I kinda figured she'd be the one, but... *really*? Do your parents know you mated with someone? Your mom is probably having a fit right about now. What did your dad say?"

Frowning at the slow-moving compact in front of me, I changed lanes and debated my answer. Might as well go with the truth. "I haven't told them yet."

Wyatt practically howled down the line, laughing his fucking head off. "You think you can keep this to yourself? You know they're going to know as soon as you walk in. You probably smell like her now. How is that honey and jasmine perfume she uses, by the way?"

At this rate, my teeth were going to be ground down to nubs. "I didn't plan on keeping it from them. It just happened so fast that I haven't had time to make a phone call. The girl that's missing? She was taken the same night of the mating, and then I was called away."

Honestly, based on Wren's reaction to me leaving, I wasn't certain she knew exactly what was happening between us. The scent of her pain was so bad, I thought I was going to keel over and die. She had to have thought I was leaving her forever to feel like that, and if that was the case...

Well, if that was the case, I was pretty sure I was screwed. But she was a Bannister witch. She was from Savannah. The Acostas and Bannisters did business from time to time—much to my mother's dismay. Most arcaners knew of wolf customs, right? They knew that the bite was as permanent as a marriage.

Didn't they?

"So that's why you're calling me instead of your family," Wyatt mused, probably petting the chia pet he called a beard as he did it, too.

"You *are* family, numb nuts. And you know damn well there is going to be an issue once they find out she's a witch. I'll be the first Acosta alpha in four hundred years not to mate another wolf. And a Bannister at that? You know damn well how fucked I am when I get home."

But I wouldn't trade it for anything—wouldn't trade *her* for anything. As much as I dragged my feet, as much as I tried to blind myself, I knew from the moment I put my hands on her that I was a goner.

"You know what I mean. I'm an Acosta wolf, but I'm not an Acosta. You have brothers. Sisters. Cousins. You could have called any one of them."

My chuckle was mirthless. "Sure, but then I'd have to explain why my entire family showed up at selection school to shadow a single Bannister witch. *You* are actually supposed to be there. You see the difference?"

"Well, you aren't wrong." Wyatt sighed like I was leeching his very soul. "Fine. I'll find a death mage to flit me over there or somethin', though you'll be responsible for the payment Simon will charge. You know how stingy he is."

That had the hair on the back of my neck prickling. "What are you doing in Tennessee?"

Simon Cartwright was the only good death mage I knew—including Girard—but his ties with the riffraff of Knoxville didn't sit so well with me. In the last year there had been a rabid shapeshifter on the loose, a whole wolf war, complete with Alpha challenge, and wolf zombies from a whacked-out death mage on a power trip.

I didn't want Wyatt anywhere near Tennessee. Plus, if Dad found out, Wyatt would be in deep shit.

"I'm not. But I do have Simon's number. He can pick me up."

Okay, one less thing to worry about.

"Good, good. Text me when you lay eyes on her." I thought about that for a second. "Please."

Wyatt's whistle rattled through my speakers. "Hoo, boy. You're going to be the worst, aren't you?"

Wincing, I shrugged, even though he couldn't see me. "Probably."

"Lucky me. Talk to you soon, man."

"Thank you, Wyatt. I mean it."

"I know you do, brother. Just try not to rip anyone's head off while you're apart. The last thing she needs is to be the one visiting you in prison."

And with that, I hung up on my best friend.

Two hours and Atlanta traffic later, I'd made it to Savannah. That was the problem with driving. I could have made it here in half the time, but even at two o'clock in the morning, Atlanta was still a fucking problem. Now it was four, I was exhausted, and I was about to run the gauntlet.

Half the lights were still on in the Acosta compound, a sprawling estate right next to Forsyth Park. The park afforded us access to a place to run, was solidly warded against humans paying us any mind, and had enough access to the historic district to make it worth it.

Savannah had a small-town feel to it, without actually being a small town. I loved it and hated it in equal measure.

Parking in the drive, I snatched my bag from the back seat and tried to go inside without anyone making a scene.

I should have known better. I barely had the front door shut before my mother was on me.

"Nicholas," my mother whispered, opening her arms wide for a hug. "I've missed you."

I'd barely set my bag down before she had me wrapped up in her arms. I would deny it to my dying day, but my mother's hugs could cure any ailment. Or I thought that a week ago. But not even my mother's hugs could cure the deep pit I had in my belly at being away from Wren.

"I was away for less than a week, Mom."

At my mother's first sniff, I tensed. When her eyes went the amber of her wolf, I braced. And when she took a few steps back and pressed both palms flat against her chest as a look of pure joy bloomed across her face, I winced.

My mother was a classic Portuguese-American woman, fiery, slightly dramatic, and loud. As a young pup, I could hear her all the way from the other end of Forsyth. But she didn't yell like she was prone to do.

No, she frowned, her expression almost hurt.

"You found your mate so soon? Why didn't you call us?" She sniffed again, longer this time. "A young woman. A w—" She slapped a hand over her mouth, her eyes going wide.

Without another word, she snatched my hand in hers and dragged me up the stairs to my father's meeting room. It was one of the twelve sound-proof rooms in the house, and the closest from the entrance. Mom closed the doors as fast as she could while I waited for the bomb to drop.

"You mated a witch, Nicholas? Are you insane?" She sniffed again.

"Would you stop that? You realize I'll tell you everything. Quit sniffing me."

Both hands found their way to her hips. Uh-oh. I was in trouble.

"Don't you take that tone with me, son. I can still take you in a challenge, and don't you forget it."

Pinching the bridge of my nose, I sighed. "Sorry, Mom, but I want to tell you about her. Not you figure it out on your own by smell alone."

She waved my words away, perching on the edge of the table. "Fine, fine. Tell me why you mated a witch and didn't tell us. I'm all ears."

"You know it doesn't work like that. I didn't get a

choice, but damn if I'd take it back now. I care about her. A lot. So I won't hear a single bad word about her, you hear me? Not one."

There were many things Catia Acosta could call herself, but "patient" hadn't ever been one of them. "Fine. I won't say a word about this witch mate you found. Can I at least get her name? What does she do? Is she from a good family? Details, son. I need the details."

"Her name is Wren, and she is from a good family. She's a probationary ABI agent going through the selection school." Vague. I would be as vague as possible, and maybe my mother would let something slide just this once.

Mom's eyebrows went up as she tapped her lip with her index finger. "Wren... I've heard that name before. What did you say her last name was again?"

No such luck. That woman did not miss a trick even at three hundred years old. She knew damn well I'd left her last name off on purpose.

"I didn't."

"Tell me her name, son."

Shaking my head, I backed away. "I'm not taking it back. It's permanent. Under the full moon of my birth, she agreed to be mine and me hers. She's my wife, Mom." Swallowing hard, I knew what she was going to say. "I'm not taking it back."

"What. Is. Her. Name."

But she already knew. I could see it in her eyes. My family didn't care for the Bannisters for several reasons, but my mother? Well, she hated Margot Bannister to the ends of the earth and maybe beyond. Not that I blamed her. Every time Wren got that broken look on her face, I wanted to rage.

"They shunned her—did you know that? They treated her like trash, like she was shit on their heel." I swallowed hard, remembering the scent of Wren's pain. Gods, it was like she was dying. Like her heart was shattering. I hated that fucking scent so much I couldn't breathe. "Do you know how much damage that woman has because of that family? How easily she believes I'll leave her? How every single kindness makes her light up with joy? You and I both know only whipped pups behave that way. You know, Mom."

I took another step back. "I'm not taking it back. She is my wife, my mate, and I'll challenge anyone who says otherwise."

A strange proudness wafted over my mother's expression. "Very good. And there is no taking it back. If you bound her as you say, then it doesn't matter what I think or who her parents are. We will welcome her as if she were one of us. Wolf or not."

I should have smelled the lie. Rookie mistake. "So, you were just fucking with me?"

My mother's laugh was an ounce of nostalgia from a happy childhood. "Sweetie, Wyatt called two hours ago to prepare me for the news. He also *may* have warned me a week ago after a human bar incident?"

Wyatt didn't have a mom. Abandoned with his father at birth, he looked to my mom a lot growing up. Hell, he was practically a member of the family. Of course he would call her.

"Really, son. Alligators?"

I still wasn't sorry about that. "They were going to rape her and who knew what else. Their pants were already unzipped, Mom."

Mom's face went green. "Wyatt seems to have left that part out. Does she know about it? Or about you hauling her out of that rattrap of an apothecary? The sheer fact the place didn't burn down twenty years ago is beyond me."

Wincing, I rubbed the back of my neck. "No. We haven't made it that far into the getting-to-know-you chats. We kind of got blindsided."

And that said nothing about the feeling in my gut when I thought about Wren's reaction to me leaving.

"Well, get some rest before you go into that infernal job of yours. Recalling you in the middle of the night?"

She shook her head. "Taking you away from your mate? Disgraceful."

Opening my arms for a hug, she moved forward into them, squeezing me like she had when I was little. "Thanks, Ma. You'll prep Dad, right?"

She planted a gentle fist into my belly. "You know I will. Your father is far more excitable than I am." *Lies.* "It just makes sense to prepare him. But tomorrow. You need your rest."

With that, I let her go, snatching my duffle from the floor and turning right to head to the East wing. Almost every unmated pack member under the age of forty lived in this house, the rest living close by within walking distance. Only my older brother Santiago and my sister Mariella were left among all the other pack youngsters. I was the youngest Acosta to find their mate in two hundred years and the first to mate outside our species in four hundred.

As soon as I brought Wren home, we would be a spectacle. She would hate it. Hell, I would, too.

But she would be here. And safe. And with me. We would be surrounded by family. I could show her what that really meant—to have a big, huge, crazy family full of people who loved you and supported you. To have unruly holiday dinners full of mundane dramas and a comforting hug when shit went sideways.

Things weren't perfect here, but it was home.

I practically fell onto my bed, clothes and all, but as comfortable as it was, rest never really found me. More than a few hours later, I was back in my truck and headed for ABI headquarters, ready to face whatever it was that was keeping me from Wren.

The place was its usual quiet. No added buzz of activity. No extra people milling around. It was early, but if I was recalled, there would have been a reason. There would have been an emergency or something.

The dread had returned, that itchy feeling between my shoulder blades that spelled danger.

Taking out my phone, I called my supervisor, Erica. Serreno was a take-no-shit elemental mage with three centuries under her belt. As high as my clearance was, Serreno's was higher since she was the acting Deputy Director of the Savannah branch. Hell, she'd even deployed to Knoxville right after they lost their own director, trying to clean the place up until the new one had taken over.

The trill of her ringtone sounded behind me, and I whipped around, ending the call. I'd called her once and left a message, but it had been after midnight, so I didn't expect her to contact me—especially if she was in need of some shut-eye in the middle of a big case. But...

"What the hell are you doing here? I thought you

were supposed to be up in Blue Ridge until June," Erica grumbled before sipping on her coffee, sweeping a long, dark twist of hair out of her eye.

My gut twisted as I plucked the folded recall orders from the folder in my hand. "I was given these at midnight. With your signature. Are you telling me I haven't been recalled back?"

Erica's frown intensified and she snatched the paper from my fingers, studying it. "I didn't sign any orders for you to return now. I don't even need you since the spike in dark magic has died down." Her gaze speared the paper as if she'd like to light it on fire. "Where the fuck did you get this?"

Girard's faking the paperwork. He faked my orders. Wren.

Wren, Wren, Wren.

"Victor Girard," I murmured, my entire body frozen for a second. "I have to go back. I have to go now."

I didn't wait for her reply. No, I ran as fast as I could on two legs, dialing Wyatt's number. He answered on the second ring. "Yeah?"

"Girard faked my orders," I growled. "Please tell me you have eyes on Wren."

"She was taking a test... that Girard was proctoring. I figured she was safe, and went to get coffee... You didn't tell me he was who you were looking out for." Wyatt paused before becoming all business. "I gotta go. I'll call you when I have eyes on our target."

Shit. Shit, fuck, cock-sucking motherfucker. Don't shift. Don't shift. Keep it together.

My truck came into view, and I jumped in, peeling out of the lot in a cloud of smoking rubber and squealing tires, steered toward the highway. I'd barely made it ten miles down the road before Wyatt called me back. I didn't even need to answer to know it was bad news, but I let him get it out, anyway.

"She's not here," he said, the regret and sorrow in his tone more than I could bear. "He's gone, too. His place is trashed. There's blood. Three kinds. Some of it's Wren's."

I couldn't even remember pulling off the side of the road. I wasn't even sure if I turned off my truck or hung up the phone. But as soon as I let the trees that lined the highway close over me, I was no longer running on two legs.

Answering my wolf's call, I landed on four, powering north as fast as they would carry me.

CHAPTER 19

WREN

Waking up shouldn't hurt this bad.

My shoulder pressed into a hard, freezing floor, the ache of it reaching its dreadful fingers up my neck and down my arm. The arm itself was asleep, so I had to have been here for a while. The shivering made my head throb, but I was so cold, I couldn't stop.

It felt like someone was driving an icepick into my brain.

"Wren?" a soft voice called. A familiar voice. "Wren, sweetie, you have to be quiet, or he'll know you're awake."

Quiet?

Then I heard it. The faint mewling of an injured animal. Only the animal in question was me. Swallowing hard, I tried to shut up, but I was only margin-ally successful.

"Fiona?" I croaked, happy as hell to know she was alive, and pissed as fuck I was in no place to offer her any assistance.

A frigid hand brushed hair from my face, and I chanced opening my eyes. The room swam as that icepick got a bit more aggressive in my noggin, but I was able to focus on her face. Fi's nose was puffy, a crust of dark red around both nostrils. One eye sported dark-purple bruising, the lid half-closed from the swelling.

He'd hit her hard. In his cabin, maybe? Had it been her blood on those papers? Had she fought back? Was that why he'd hit her?

"Found you," I whispered, trying to sit up. Only one arm worked, and it was weak, but I managed to slowly take the pressure off the aching shoulder. Pins and needles flooded the dead limb.

"Yeah, sweetheart. You found me. Though, I have to say I rather wished you would have brought the cavalry with you."

Yeah, me too.

"Well, the goal was to find out whether or not you were actually missing, so... Mission accomplished?"

Fiona's chuckle was mirthless and then her bottom lip wobbled. "It was Girard. You know that, right?"

I nodded and immediately regretted it. Nausea twisted my stomach and I prayed I wouldn't vomit. "Yeah," I croaked. "I kind of figured. He's the one who said you'd terminated your contract and left."

Fiona's good eye sparked with rage. "'Terminated' my contract?" she hissed, using air quotes and everything. But those air quotes made me realize why we were sitting on the floor. Fiona's wrist was cuffed, the manacle attached to a long chain that was secured to the floor by a solid-looking eye-ring. And there was another chain, but unlike Fiona's, mine was attached to my very bare ankle.

Shit.

"More like he kidnapped me in the middle of the night, the bastard." She shook her head, an action I envied at the moment. "Though, he didn't mean to nab me. When you left, I sort of figured you were off to see Instructor Smexy Pants, so I stuffed pillows under my blankets and then went to sleep in your bed."

"What?" My stomach pitched, nearly making the contents revolt.

She shrugged. "I figured if Ames walked into our cabin or somethin' and he saw 'you' in bed, he'd leave, and no one would know you'd been gone."

Man, how I wished she wouldn't have done that. It was fucking sweet and probably one of the kinder things someone had done for me, but given our current predicament...

"Didn't that just come to bite me in the ass?"

"I'm so sorry, Fi."

She waved my apology away like she wouldn't hear of it. "*You* didn't take me from my nice, warm bed. *You* didn't spirit me off using some awful death magic, hopping through shadows like a wonky tilt-a-whirl. *You* didn't sock me in the nose and then blindfold my ass and try to sell me on the black fucking market."

The cabin tilted a little bit, the rough planked walls letting dim light and a bitter wind through. "What?"

There was a black market? A black market? For selling people?

And Girard had meant to sell *me*. My heart started beating out of my chest, and a warm trickle of wetness seeped down the back of my head.

Please be sweat, please be sweat, please be sweat.

I reached for the wetness and my fingers came away red, and the room spun a bit more.

"Yeah. Only when Girard took me to his buyer, the guy said I wasn't who he asked for and wouldn't take me." Fi paused, letting out another mirthless laugh. "You know, I'm not sure if I should be grateful or offended. Obviously, I don't wanna be sold, but I'm from top-notch stock." She blew a raspberry, tossing her hair halfheartedly. "I'm a fucking delight, dammit."

"Right?" I agreed, trying not to nod as I chuckled. How Fiona could keep her head like this was a damn mystery, but I was all for it. But her tale had me wondering if all the women taken from the selection school had been sold like commodities by Girard.

It made me wish I would have known this place was so dangerous. It made me want better for us all.

And it made me fucking mad.

But all that anger, it fled my body as soon as footsteps clomped outside.

Fiona's gaze widened just like mine likely did. She mouthed a silent, "Pretend to be asleep," and I dropped to the floor, hurting my pins-and-needles arm and jostling my head. Closing my eyes, I caught one last glimpse of her frightened expression before darkness overtook me.

The door complained as it opened, the loud screeching nearly making me jump. Attempting to be as still as possible, I barely breathed while the boots plodded closer, each step adding to the dread in my chest.

Would Nico come looking after Hannah lost me? Would he blame her? And how would he find us? Girard likely covered his scent when he took me just like he'd done with Fiona. And where were we? By the state of this shack, we could be anywhere from northern Georgia to fucking Canada for all I knew.

Think, Wren.

But thinking was hard. My head hurt and I couldn't see anything, and Girard probably had a gazillion years on me. What the fuck was I going to do that he hadn't already thought of?

It turned out our deception was for nothing. After a few long moments of tense silence while I poorly attempted to feign unconsciousness, a hard grip found my shoulders and hauled my upper body off the floor, slamming me into the rickety wall. Even though said wall was no more than a foot away, my whole body revolted at the motion, nearly making me vomit.

Girard's steel-gray eyes glowed with his power, focusing right on me. Cupping my chin, he squeezed my cheeks with his long-fingered hand. But old Girard had seen better days. The long hair he usually kept in a bun or queue at his nape, was loose and wild like he'd run backward through a bush. His beard was bushy and unkempt, his nose bloody, and he had three thick scratches on one cheek as if someone had taken their nails to him.

Fiona maybe?

"Well, well, well. Aren't you the biggest fucking pain in the ass?"

Jerking my chin out of his hand made my head feel like it was going to explode, but I didn't want his stale breath in my face or his slimy touch on my skin.

"I'm sorry," I said, sneering. "I didn't mean to get in the middle of your black-market trafficking racket. So sorry to inconvenience you. What was I thinking?"

This time Girard latched onto my throat, lifting me off the ground like I weighed nothing. "Does Acosta like that smart mouth of yours? Or does he shove his dick down your throat to keep you quiet?" He held me up off the floor, my toes scrabbling for purchase but finding nothing as I struggled to breathe. "What? No witty comeback?"

Then he dropped me, my ankle taking the brunt of the fall. That time, I did vomit, losing my meager breakfast on the rough wood floor.

Too bad I missed his boots. *The fucker.*

"Disgusting," he hissed, shuffling back to avoid my mess. "What they see in you, I'll never know. Maybe Ames was right about you."

"Fuck. You," I gasped, wiping my mouth of spittle and grossness.

Girard knelt, examining me like a side of beef. "No thanks. You belong to someone else. Bought and paid for already. Though, I should charge Desmond extra for as much trouble as you've been."

Desmond? Is that who he plans on selling me to?

"And you," he barked, giving Fiona a disgusted scowl. "What am I going to do with you? Desmond doesn't want you, you've seen too much already, and making you forget is tricky. It'd be easier to just kill you, but I'm not too keen on getting my hands dirty."

"Oh, poor you," I growled, repulsed after everything I'd been through, I was about to be bested by a man without an inch of sack. Fabulous. "It's not like you're being sold, so fuck everyone else, right? How many women have you pawned off to—Desmond, was it? How many? Ten? Fifty? A hundred?"

Girard whipped out a hand, slamming into my cheek with enough force to split my lip and nearly knock me unconscious. "Everything would have been a lot easier if Desmond would have just snagged you at that stupid apothecary. But *noooooo*. Pretty boy Acosta got in the way." He stood, pacing back and forth over the warped wooden planks. "He enlisted me to nab you, but lo and behold Acosta gets in the way again. Did you know your boyfriend has already killed for you? I bet you think it's real sweet."

Killed for me? Excuse me? "What?"

"Oh, he didn't tell you? That's rich. The wolf prince

doesn't want his lady love to know about the blood on his hands, I bet. You went out drinking with your friend, and I paid two humans to bring you to me. They met a nasty end out in the swamp, but I had a backup. But every single time, he was with you or watching you or fucking you. Really. Does the man even let you pee by yourself?"

Wait. Girard said the apothecary. Nico was the man that got me out? He's known about me this whole time?

"It's cute how little you know. Maybe Desmond will make you his little pet. Put you on a leash and parade you around the Fae court. All that wide-eyed innocence will get stomped out in a week."

I thought about telling Girard to go fuck himself, but I didn't have a whole lot of consciousness left under my belt, and I couldn't figure out our escape if I was knocked out.

"You got a lot of nerve," Fiona began, spearing him with her fiery blue gaze. "You know who I am, and you still want to kill me? Darlin', I don't know if you're brave or stupid." She clucked her tongue like a good Southern woman and shook her head. "Now, my daddy and I don't quite get along, but I'll bet every shoe I have in my closet he'll give a damn if some two-bit death mage takes out his only daughter."

Girard scoffed, standing so he could glare down at

her. "They won't find out, but why would I give a damn about some backwoods witch coven?"

Fiona stared at him like he was two bushels shy of a full load. "I'm a *Jacobs*, you dumb bitch. Josiah Jacobs' only daughter." She raised her eyebrows, waiting for him to get it. Hell, even I got it, and I was so far removed from the arcane world it was silly.

Josiah Jacobs had been implicated in several high-profile murders, but no one could ever make the charges stick. Under his iron fist, the Jacobs coven had reached infamous status, with few willing to go against them. They weren't all bad. They took care of their own, and didn't make waves unless you got on their bad side. But oh, if you did...

Understanding dawned on Girard's face.

"There you go, Sugar Plum. Now you're getting it." She crossed her arms over her chest and leaned against the wall like she wasn't chained or bloody or freezing. "So that puts you between a rock and a hard place. You've got an Acosta on your ass for taking his girl, the whole of the Jacobs coven ready and willing to go to war at a moment's notice, and a Fae deal hanging in the balance. It *is* a Fae deal, right?"

At Girard's continued silence, she pressed forward. "So, breaking a Fae deal has consequences, and no one wants to do that, but is there a loophole? Why don't you think about it real hard, save your backside, and make me an offer?"

Girard's smile was snide, as a black ball of magic formed in his hand. It was putrid stuff, trailing down his arm and up his fingers. Oily and slick and made of death. "I think I'll just kill you instead."

Until that very moment, I'd forgotten about the amulet that hung around my neck. But as soon as I saw that magic, it reminded me of just how destructive I could be.

Just how deadly.

Because as soon as that ball formed in his hand, I knew our only option was the fucked-up magic that ran in my veins. The awful curse that made every spell backfire. That made every power fizzle and burn and explode.

Before he let loose that putrid orb of darkness, I fisted my hand over the chain and yanked, tossing the amulet as far away from me as the little cabin could provide.

Then everything seemed to happen at once. Fire bloomed in Girard's palm, the dark magic transforming on a dime. He screamed in pain as a force blew him backward into the shack's wall. And just like in that damn apothecary, the flames only grew, jumping from one plank to the next like a brushfire.

Fiona wasted no time, she stood, gripping both sides of the chain and ripping it up, yanking the eye hook out of the wood with her bare hands.

She held out a hand. "Come on."

Shakily, I got to my feet, and Fiona half-dragged, half-carried me out of there. She shouldered through the rickety door, hauling my ass behind her as we stepped out into the light. But what we found was little better than the cabin. As far as the eye could see there was nothing but trees. No buildings. No town.

Just more and more trees.

Fiona and I were both broken, both barefoot, and even in the back half of May, there was snow on the ground of this godforsaken forest. Still, Fi took off, dragging me along as she led us out of there. My ankle protested, my head throbbed, but I followed her down the slope like she knew where she was going.

All the while, we heard Girard's screams as he burned. Only... they seemed to be getting closer.

Then I knew.

I hadn't killed him.

Girard was alive.

And he was very, very pissed off.

CHAPTER 20
NICO

She's bleeding.

S I stared at Wren's blood puddled on Girard's floor and made a decision. I was going to murder Victor Girard the first chance I got and there was not a damn thing anyone could do to stop me.

Two hours of straight running had landed me back at the selection school deep in the Blue Ridge Mountains, but even that scant bit of time had been far too late. Wyatt had corralled the students to search the woods for Wren, for Girard. All the shifters had been given her scent and a job to do. Even Ames was looking for her.

But Wren was still gone, and I needed more help than I had to find her.

She's bleeding. She's out there bleeding somewhere.

"I need you to get it together, Malia. That big puddle of blood right there," I barked, pointing at the dark burgundy stain on Girard's wood floor, "is the best fucking clue I got in the middle of this shit. So, I'm going to need you to gather whatever gifts you have, and fucking find her."

Malia Nadir was a gifted psychometry witch. Unable to cast a single spell, but she was more than gifted when it came to gleaning information from objects. Nadir wasn't the first one I'd come across either, and often-times, it was possible for them to find someone in the future.

If they just fucking looked hard enough.

"And I told you five times already that I can't do it. I get all the past shit. Her life, what she was thinking when she lost the blood, whatever. But I can't get her future—not because I don't have the *ability*, but because something is *blocking* me. So throw your hissy fit some-where else."

I didn't know what else to try. None of the psychics I knew could help with a witch they didn't know, and even if Wren had a few in her family, I doubted they would step up. What I needed was information, and I wasn't above doing shady shit to get it, either.

She's bleeding.

I had a feeling I knew exactly what was blocking

Nadir's ability, too, and it was the same damn thing that made it so I couldn't find her, either.

That fucking necklace.

I'd been so proud of myself for getting Carmichael to make it for her, thinking it would be the perfect thing to keep her safe. Now she was alone with a death mage who had a history of taking women. She was hurt. And if she was still in these mountains, she had to be cold. A freak storm had been brewing over the last few hours, spitting snow even down here. The higher peaks were likely getting hammered or worse.

She's bleeding.

"Then I need someone—anyone—to think of something because I swear to everything I find holy, if something happens to her, I will rain down Hell itself," I warned through gritted teeth. "You hear me, Ames," I shouted through the door and the absolute moron who hadn't realized until an hour ago that Girard had been feeding rumors to the students to frame his idiot ass and keep himself out of the hotseat. "Work whatever magic you got before I lose my fucking patience."

"I've tried every locator spell on this planet, you prick," he fired back, kicking the door open. "I'm getting stonewalled. Maybe if you'd have told someone that she was a goddamned amplifier, you wouldn't have needed to slap a Band-Aid null ward around her neck that blocks us all."

I'd had to come clean about that, but I informed the warlock that if he told anyone, I would rip his balls off and shove them down his throat.

"Maybe if *anyone* would have said something, we could have gotten her the help she needed."

"Oh, that's rich," Malia hissed, staring at Ames like he was a steaming pile of dog shit. "This coming from the same guy who slandered her name every chance he got. Who threatened to kick her out at every turn. Who hounded her ass and asked if she was going to fuck you for a good grade. Eat shit, you prick. You never wanted to help her. Don't try to paint yourself as the good guy now that she's gone."

Asked if she was going to fuck you for a good grade.

Wyatt slapped a hand on my shoulder, keeping me from killing the useless sack of shit. That was okay. As soon as I got Ames alone, it would be all over. But finding Wren mattered more.

"You do realize your days are numbered, right?" Wyatt said without a lick of anger or even so much as a frown. "You messed with an alpha's mate. I suggest you make right with whatever god you call holy before he rips you apart."

While that was most definitely true, I needed everyone to fucking focus. "What I need is for all of us to *think*. If Girard had to stash someone for a little while in the middle of this storm, where would he go? Does he have a house somewhere?" I growled, trying to stay on task. "Any friends with a property? Did he talk about needing to get away or having money trouble? Something?"

Wyatt snorted a laugh. "You don't know Girard very well. He doesn't talk to us if he can help it."

Fucking perfect.

If Wren were a wolf, she could have protected herself. If she were a wolf, I would know where she was because all wolves were connected. I would know if she was alive. I would...

After four hundred years of not a single wolf being mated outside of the species, and I was the one with the danger-prone mate who I couldn't fucking find.

Then in a single instant everything changed.

One second, I was fine—pissed, worried out of my mind, but fine—and the next, I could barely stand. It felt like an icepick had been rammed into my eye as my gut twisted, and I nearly fell to my knees. My ankle throbbed, and my lungs were on fire.

And I was scared—more scared than I'd ever been in my life.

But none of it felt like my pain, my fear, my exhaustion.

Gods, was this...

Was this Wren?

Mated wolves didn't work like this. Only our wolves were connected. This was—

Flashes of trees filtered into my mind, the pain of seeing them nearly splitting my skull. "Touch the blood," I gasped, trying not to keel over. "Do it."

Malia slammed her palm into the drying liquid, her amber eyes milking over as she searched for Wren once more. "She's running barefoot. With Fiona. Forest. There's snow on the ground. Not far. Past camp. Past the null line. Girard's chasing them." Malia paused, her breaths coming in pants like mine, likely feeling that same splitting agony in her skull. "She's hurt, Acosta."

But I didn't need Malia to tell me that. I knew it better than my own name at this point.

My mate was running barefoot in the snow to outrun her captor, and I was already turning, running, my feet taking me to her as I stumbled out of the cabin and up the hill. Wren was north in a place in the mountains where there was a decent amount of snow on the ground.

And then I was no longer on two feet, I was on four, racing up the mountain to find her. A moment later,

Wyatt was at my flank. The screech of a bird up ahead called to me, almost begging me to follow it, and gods help me, I did.

My vision blurred as Wren's mind brought a cliff into view. I knew that outcropping. We'd been there during Hell Night, and I had to direct the cadets farther west so they wouldn't get past the null line.

Veering east, I picked up the pace, racing for Wren as if both our lives depended on it.

Because they did.

Gasping, I landed on my hands and knees, trying to suck in a single full breath.

"Come on, Wren," Fi wheezed, her breathing no better than mine. "I need you to get up."

Fiona and I were chained together. No way could she carry us both. Not after a day with no food or water or sleep. But the world was swimming, and my lungs were burning, and my ankle wasn't going to hold my weight for much longer. And that snow on the ground? Well, with the storm clouds churning overhead, we were in for a fuck-ton more of it.

But living was more important than pain, so I stood up, ready to get moving again. Girard's screams had quieted but he was still stomping through the forest, the cracks of branches snapping beneath his feet made me jump every time. He was getting closer, and we didn't have time to fuck around.

Nodding, I took some of the chain's slack, wrapping it around my left arm so she didn't have to carry it all. We needed to keep moving.

Fiona took two steps right, and then it didn't matter if either of us were walking, because she was falling down a sharp decline. And since we were chained together, I was, too.

Rocks battered my skin as we skidded down the slope, a very real cliff rocketing toward us at breakneck speed. I scrabbled for purchase, grasping at anything that would keep us from sliding off this fucking, gods-forsaken mountain. My shoulder slammed into a rock, then my head, then it was sort of lights out for a second.

By some miracle, the chain itself caught on a boulder, yanking the both of us to a stop.

The metal cut into my arm and hand, and I immediately regretted trying to pick up the slack.

"Fi?" I called and instantly started coughing, the dirt and dust of our slide filling my lungs.

Her answering cough was music to my ears.

"I'm alive," she choked. "Maybe that rest was a better idea, yeah?"

Half-coughing, half-laughing, I assessed the beautiful, lovely, awesome rock that stopped us from tumbling off a fucking mountain.

"You got a hold on something?" I asked, really hoping she did. If I stayed here any longer, I was going to lose feeling in my arm, and that was most likely a very bad thing.

"Yeah, I got a root here, and the slope flattens out a bit before the drop. We can slide down slow and get our bearings."

And all we had to do was pray to the gods that Girard didn't look too close at this ridge or was temporarily deaf while we screamed down the side of a fucking mountain.

Sure. Totally plausible.

Groaning, I braced my feet and tried inching the chain off the rock bit by bit. But as much as I struggled, the chain just wouldn't budge, caught on something...

Then the unmistakable sound of heavy footfalls reached my ears, and I froze, trying to plaster myself to the side of the slope.

"You can't hide from me," Girard shouted from above. "I know you're down there."

Fiona scrambled up, trying to help me disengage the damn chain, but Girard was a fuck of a lot faster than either of us. In a swath of black smoke, he appeared right in front of us, wrapping his burned and weeping hands around our throats.

And then it felt as if my whole body was being turned inside out. The world spun at hyper speed as darkness cloaked me. I wanted to scream, cry, something, but all I could do was stand there while he seemed to yank me from space and time and deposit me somewhere else.

The "somewhere else" was nothing more than the outcropping where we fell, and Girard screamed in agony as all three of us dropped to the dirt.

"Didn't learn your lesson the first time, huh?" I croaked after spitting out a mouthful of dirt and blood. "You can't use magic on me, stupid."

"I sort of figured he'd learn the first time, but as my daddy always says, you can't fix stupid," Fiona rasped, cradling her cuffed arm against her chest.

Girard's charred face whipped to us. His beard was mostly burned away as was a good chunk of his long hair. One eye was crusted shut, but the other gleamed with hatred. "I'm going to fucking kill you, you bitch. I'll kill you both."

"Go ahead and try, sport," I growled, staggering to my feet as I twisted the slack of the chain around my bloody hand. I wasn't quite sure what I was going to do with that chain other than wrap it around his fucking neck and pull, but I was damn sure I'd manage. "I fucking dare you."

Could he kick my ass? Absolutely. But I wouldn't cower, and I sure as *shit* wouldn't let him sell me to some Fae dickwad. Girard could eat this fucking chain and like it.

Then Girard's face went white as he took a big step back. And the best sound I'd ever heard in my entire life rumbled from right behind me. Not one, but two wolves growled, adding a level of backup I'd never had. Up above, a bird screeched, before diving for Girard. Its claws raked his face before flitting away, and he stumbled back a step, inching closer to that slippery fucking slope.

A cloud of gray smoke engulfed the bird, and then it wasn't a bird anymore. It was Gianna, with her odd yellow eyes, and a pair of daggers in her hands.

Before Girard could go over the side, Nico was on him, jumping from four feet to two in the span of a single blink. In human form, he vibrated with rage, his clawed hand digging into the skin of that asshole's neck. One flick of his fingers and Girard would be worm food.

Nico didn't say a word in threat—he didn't have to —his face said everything, but Girard would *not* shut up. "Yo-you can't kill me, Acosta. Think about the law."

Nico's smile was feral. "You broke the law already. No one will give two shits if I rip your throat out. Preventing a murder and all that."

Girard's lone working eye widened. "Yo-you need me. I can give you Desmond. I can give you my buyer."

Nico flinched like Girard had struck him. "Buyer?"

"You think I killed all those girls? I'm not a murderer. I'm a businessman," Girard wheedled.

Like that would do him any favors.

"He's leaving a big part out," I rasped, my voice like I'd swallowed glass. "Desmond? His buyer? Is a Fae." And if Girard had made a deal with the Fae, there was no way he'd tell anyone anything about it.

Even I knew that.

Girard's eye went even wider. "I'll tell you everything I can. I *swear*."

Nico's lip curled as his fingers tightened on Girard's neck. "That's good to hear, Girard. But there's just one problem." He brought the death mage closer to his face and whispered, "I don't believe you."

Without hesitation, Nico slashed, ripping out Girard's throat as if it were a knife through butter. The older man fell, shock coloring his features before going slack, landing on the dirt like a sack of rotten potatoes.

It was bad that I wasn't sorry, right? That I

witnessed that death and didn't even flinch, didn't gasp. That I was glad Girard was gone.

"Wren?" Nico murmured, and I blinked. Somehow, he was right in front of me. I was so busy staring at Girard bleeding out, that I didn't even notice when Nico had gotten there. "Beautiful?"

Then the shivers came flooding back as everything started crashing over me. The adrenaline, the fear, the rage… "Look, Fi. I brought the cavalry after all."

By the time Nico, his friend, Wyatt, and Gianna got Fiona and I down the mountain, the storm that had been swirling over our heads broke, dumping a mountain's worth of snow all over everything.

Currently stuffed under three blankets, a heating pad, and drinking a mug full of hot apple cider, I rested on Nico's—or rather *Wyatt's*—couch, answering questions from Deputy Director Serreno. Evidently, she had wasted no time following Nico up here after his abrupt departure, arriving along with a small contingent of agents just before the storm.

Nico had perched himself next to me, resting my legs on his lap as he rubbed my ankle and held my hand for all and sundry to see. Serreno was kind to me—to us both—telling me to call her Erica, but her questions made me want to burrow under the blankets and not come out for about a decade.

"Please tell me why you thought it was appropriate to break into Commandant Girard's home. Why did you feel that was necessary?"

Nico growled long and low, shooting me a look that promised we would talk about this later.

See? Definitely wanted to hide.

"I felt that if I could procure evidence that proved Girard fabricated Jacobs' paperwork, then an investigation could begin into the uncounted number of missing probationary and field agents. And according to Section 12.4.5908B, any concrete information brought to an agent must be investigated regardless of where it came from. Since I am not technically a member of the ABI until graduation, I could pass it off to an agent I trusted without breaking any laws." I swallowed hard, watching her eyebrows climb up her forehead.

"Other than breaking and entering, you mean," she murmured, poking a hole in my ABI law research. Luckily, I had a backup.

Swallowing, I continued, "And—"

"Oh, goodie," Nico groused. "There's more."

I shot him a glare. "*And* based off of Section 56.9.5732G, it is legal for any agent or civilian to enter the home of a suspected criminal uninvited if they fear an arcaner's life is in jeopardy. Since Commandant Girard threatened to murder Cadet Jacobs, I feel this qualifies under that statute. So..."

Nico twisted in his seat, his glare boring a hole in the side of my face. I sipped my cider and waited.

"You memorized the ABI statutes?" Serreno asked, her eyebrows not coming down anytime soon. "All of them?"

"Sort of," I mumbled into my mug. "I kind of thought we were supposed to know the law if we were going to enforce the law. And..." I shrugged, trying not to wince. "And I didn't want to get kicked out of here since it's a death sentence if I don't pass."

Serreno sat back in her seat. "What?"

Nico nodded. "According to her paperwork, she is recommended for execution if she cannot complete the course. I read it myself." He moved my feet off his lap and stood. "So if you plan on kicking her out, you're going to have to go through the entire Acosta pack. Just putting that out there."

Serreno blinked and then smiled huge. "So noted."

"Get out of my way right this instant," a shrill, and yet oh-so-familiar voice demanded right outside Nico's cabin before the formidable redhead burst through the door.

Eloise Bannister may have been a grandmother several times over, but her hair was as red as mine, her skin ageless, and her spine as straight as an arrow. And if the world could have let me melt through this couch and hide, that would have been awesome.

She took one look at my battered face, my blankets, and my cider, and her lip curled. "*Wren.*"

Just my name was a chastisement and a good one at that.

"Embarrassing the family name yet again, I see. Get up from that couch, girl. You're going home with me."

Nico squared off against my grandmother, and Serreno stood as well. But it was Nico who spoke first.

"The fuck she will. Wren isn't going anywhere near your family ever again. Not if I can help it."

Eloise startled, her disgust shifting to Nico. "You think that pelt of yours means something to me? Who do you think you are, wolf?"

Nico bristled, his eyes glowing, his fangs lengthening, his claws erupting from his fingertips. Long and low, he growled, before stating something that damn near knocked me off the couch.

"I'm her fucking husband. And you'll take her from me over my cold, dead body."

Umm, what?

I must have said that out loud because Nico turned, staring at me with all the truth and hope in his eyes.

We were married. His face said it all. In some weird wolfy way, he considered us married.

Holy.

Shit.

And if Nico's face was awash in hope, my grand-mother's said she would greatly appreciate Nico's dead body on a silver platter.

And just like when he'd pulled me from those flames in that stupid apothecary, I was once again elbow-deep in shit.

What else was new?

Thank you so much for reading Spells & Slip-ups. I can't express just how much I love Wren & Nico and their ragtag bunch of friends. And we aren't quite done yet!

*Next up is **Magic & Mayhem** and all the crazy, witchy shenanigans that is to come. I hope you're buckled in to see Wren & Nico contend with the Arcane Bureau of Investigation and her faulty powers... oh, and their crazy mate bond!*

GET IT NOW!

Want the skinny on future releases without having to follow me absolutely everywhere on social media?

Text "LEGION" to (844) 311-5791

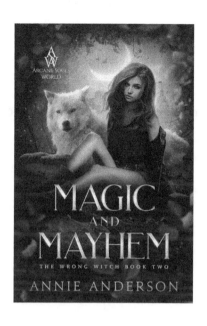

MAGIC & MAYHEM

The Wrong Witch Book Two

All it took was one bite.

A week ago, I was the perpetual screw up of the
Bannister coven and a probationary agent for the
Arcane Bureau of Investigation. Somehow, I've
managed to get myself mated to an Acosta alpha, pissed
off my family, and gotten on the radar of a dark Fae.

As much as I'd like to bury my head in the sand, I have a
badge to secure—and with a new case on my proverbial

desk—a job to do. Because I'm not the first witch that the Fae has tried to steal, but I will definitely be the last.

Just as soon as I get this curse under control...

Get your copy today!

BOOKS BY ANNIE ANDERSON

SEVERED FLAMES

Ruined Wings

Stolen Embers

Broken Fates

IMMORTAL VICES & VIRTUES

HER MONSTROUS MATES

Bury Me

SHADOW SHIFTER BONDS

Shadow Me

THE ARCANE SOULS WORLD

GRAVE TALKER SERIES

Dead to Me

Dead & Gone

Dead Calm

Dead Shift

Dead Ahead

Dead Wrong

Dead & Buried

SOUL READER SERIES

Night Watch

Death Watch

Grave Watch

THE WRONG WITCH SERIES

Spells & Slip-ups

Magic & Mayhem

Errors & Exorcisms

THE LOST WITCH SERIES

Curses & Chaos

Hexes & Hijinx

THE ETHEREAL WORLD

PHOENIX RISING SERIES

(Formerly the Ashes to Ashes Series)

Flame Kissed

JOIN THE LEGION

EXCLUSIVE SNEAK PEEKS,
GIVEAWAYS, BOOK DISCUSSION.
COME FOR THE BOOKS.
STAY FOR THE MEMES.

To stay up to date on all things Annie Anderson, get exclusive access to ARCs and giveaways, and be a member of a fun, positive, drama-free space, join The Legion!

facebook.com/groups/ThePhoenixLegion

Acknowledgments

A huge, honking thank you to Shawn, Barb, Jade, Angela, Heather, Kelly, Erin, and April. Thanks for the late-night calls, the endurance of my whining, the incessant plotting sessions, the wine runs...

Basically, thanks for putting up with my bullshit.

Every single one of you rock and I couldn't have done it without you.

About the Author

Annie Anderson is the author of the international best-selling Rogue Ethereal series. A United States Air Force veteran, Annie pens fast-paced Urban Fantasy novels filled with strong, snarky heroines and a boatload of magic. When she takes a break from writing, she can be found binge-watching The Magicians, flirting with her husband, wrangling children, or bribing her cantankerous dogs to go on a walk.

To find out more about Annie and her books, visit www.annieande.com

facebook.com/AuthorAnnieAnderson

instagram.com/AnnieAnde

amazon.com/author/annieande

bookbub.com/authors/annie-anderson

goodreads.com/AnnieAnde

pinterest.com/annieande

tiktok.com/@authorannieanderson